Stolen from her family

Mr. Thomas grabbed me and flung me over his shoulder like a sack of corn. I pummeled him with my fists, kicked, and tried to bite him. Although I was nearly thirteen, I was slightly built and no match for someone twice my size, especially as I was hanging upside down.

He turned and spoke to Mother.

"We came for Captain Wakefield but shall take what we can get. Tell your husband he may redeem his daughter from the British garrison at Lloyd's Neck."

Then he strode out of the yard into the darkness.

"No!" Mother cried out. And I raised my head to see her running toward me.

Percy intercepted her and brought his pistol to her head.

"Do not follow," he growled.

"Hope exhibits tremendous resourcefulness and steadfastness. . . . She learns that the enemy wears a very human face. This story is rich with the details of life during the Revolutionary War."
—*School Library Journal*

OTHER PUFFIN BOOKS YOU MAY ENJOY

Hope's Crossing

Joan Elizabeth Goodman

PUFFIN BOOKS

PUFFIN BOOKS
Published by the Penguin Group
Penguin Putnam Books for Young Readers,
345 Hudson Street, New York, New York 10014, U.S.A.
Penguin Books Ltd, 27 Wrights Lane, London W8 5TZ, England
Penguin Books Australia Ltd, Ringwood, Victoria, Australia
Penguin Books Canada Ltd, 10 Alcorn Avenue, Toronto, Ontario, Canada M4V 3B2
Penguin Books (N.Z.) Ltd, 182-190 Wairau Road, Auckland 10, New Zealand

Penguin Books Ltd, Registered Offices: Harmondsworth, Middlesex, England

First published in the United States of America by Houghton Mifflin Company, 1998
Published by Puffin Books,
a member of Penguin Putnam Books for Young Readers, 1999

1 3 5 7 9 10 8 6 4 2

LIBRARY OF CONGRESS CATALOGING-IN-PUBLICATION DATA
Goodman, Joan E.
Hope's crossing / Joan Elizabeth Goodman.
p. cm.
Summary: During the Revolutionary War, thirteen-year-old Hope, seized by the band of
Tories who attack her Connecticut home, finds herself enslaved in a Tory household on
Long Island and uses all her resources to escape from her captors and make her way home.
ISBN 0-698-11807-3 (pbk.)
1. New York (State)—History—Revolution, 1775–1763 Juvenile Fiction. [1. New York
(State)—History—Revolution, 1775–1763 Fiction. 2. United States—History—Revolution,
1775–1783 Fiction. 3. Courage Fiction.] I. Title.
PZ7.G61375Ho 1999 [Fic]—dc21 99-21470 CIP

Printed in the United States of America

Acknowledgments

I'd especially like to thank Thomas Kuehhas, of the Oyster Bay Historical Society, Barbara Austen, of the Fairfield Historical Society, and my nautical consultant, Ted Danforth, for their help. However, any errors in the text are mine, not theirs.

Dedication

For Matilda W. Welter, Margaret Gabel,
and Robin Rue, the guardian angels of this book

Contents

Preface

During the Revolutionary War, small parties of raiders from Long Island terrorized the coast of Connecticut. "During June of 1777, Long Island loyalists raided and burned the home of William Palmer of Mill River. They took Palmer's daughter, Mary, when they departed, but Captain Amos Perry, Palmer's neighbor, overtook the raiders before they reached New York, rescued Mary and captured their vessel."*

Hope Wakeman was not so fortunate.

*from Thomas J. Farnham, *Fairfield: The Biography of a Community 1639–1989* (The Fairfield Historical Society, 1988).

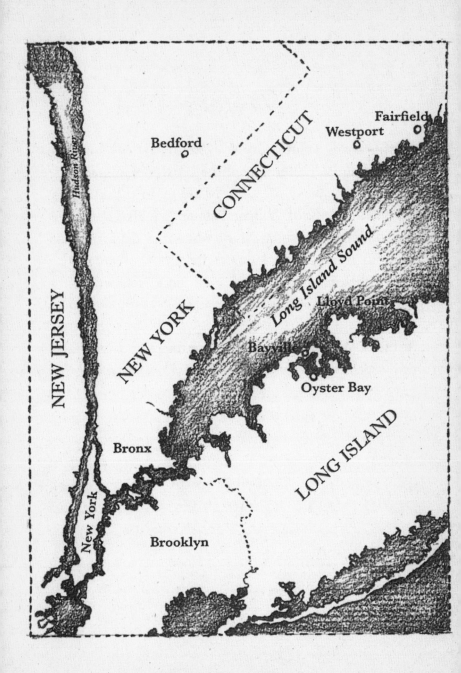

I

'Tis War, Mistress!

They came one moonless night in November. The dogs heard them and set to barking, but no one who could save us was there to hear. I had woken before our dogs, knowing something was terribly wrong. My first thoughts were for Father, gone a fortnight on General Washington's orders. Was he in danger? Had he been wounded? Or was it Mother? She'd been so low since the birth of Jonathan. With the sudden departure of Father, her spirits had sunk further. Was she worse? And the babe, himself so small and weak, had he sickened? Until Jack and Jubal started barking I'd had no fears for myself.

Yet I had plenty of reason to fear. Mother, Jonathan, my little sisters, and I were alone with the two serving girls. We had no near neighbors. Uncle Seldon had gone to General Washington soon after Father. Peter, our hired hand, had been sent to help on Grandfather Wakeman's farm. We had nothing but faith to protect us.

Seconds later, there was a loud wrenching sound and crash as they broke down the front door. Heavy footsteps pounded up the stairs. Mother screamed from her bedroom, and Jonathan commenced to wail.

Redcoats! I thought. The British army has landed, and we shall all die.

My little sisters, Mary and Abigail, slept soundly on as they had often slept through the most tempestuous summer storms. I wished I could be that safe asleep, but I had to go to Mother. I couldn't let her face the soldiers with only Jonathan for comfort. I left my bed and crept down the hall to Mother's room.

To begin with I was relieved. These weren't soldiers in uniform; they might have been some of our Fairfield neighbors. They were dressed like the ragtag farmers or merchantmen hereabouts. Perhaps they were militiamen with some message from Father. But when the tall, dark-haired man spoke I realized that they were strangers and their errand was in no way neighborly. These men were our sworn enemies — Tory raiders — come from Long Island with the tide.

"Where is Captain Wakeman?" he demanded.

Mother was too frightened to do more than weep.

"Speak, mistress!"

"Mercy," cried Mother, holding Jonathan to her breast. "Mercy!"

The tall man looked as if he would strike her. I slipped through the men to Mother's side. She pulled me close to her and continued to sob.

"Father is gone," I said.

"Where?" He loomed over me, while the other men regarded me, grim-faced.

"G-g-gone to General Washington."

"More like he is hiding in the hay or the root cellar," said the fat man, who was holding a pistol. "Do not tell us tales, missy."

"It's true," I said. "Father's been gone a fortnight."

"But Mr. Thomas, you said Captain Wakeman was still in Fairfield," said the skinny man in a long, greasy coat.

Mr. Thomas glared at me even as he answered the skinny man.

"That was the information from the garrison at Lloyd's Neck," he said, daring me to contradict him.

"He meant to stay longer, he had another month's leave," I said, and my words came out in little pitiful squeaks. "But a message came from General Washington, and Father left the next morning."

"And where did he go?"

"Father didn't tell us."

The fat man brought his pistol level with Mother's breast. "Is that so, mistress?"

Mother nodded and sobbed.

Mr. Thomas regarded Mother and me silently for a few moments, and then he sighed.

He believed us, thank God!

"What's to be done?" asked the man with the lantern.

"We will take what we can get," said Mr. Thomas, and he laughed. In that laugh was our ruin.

The men's faces relaxed. In fact, they looked quite pleased.

"Dimon, Percy," said Mr. Thomas. "You go downstairs. See what you can find of silver or pewter. Brewster, you search the bedrooms. Mistress, you will show me Captain Wakeman's papers."

The three men left the room to ransack our house.

"Your husband's papers, Mrs. Wakeman!"

They must have been looking for information on General Washington's army to bring back to the British. Father might, indeed, have such information in his papers. Mother looked dumbly at Mr. Thomas. She seemed too afraid to understand him, too fearful to move from her spot. I could tell that he had no patience with her. And I spoke up before he could harm her.

"Father's papers will be in his desk in the parlor. The key should be here in this clothespress." Whatever secrets Father might have wouldn't be kept in his desk, but well hidden.

"Get it," said Mr. Thomas. "And be quick!"

I went to the clothespress, my hand fumbling with the latch, and began searching clumsily through Father's things. Here was a woolen vest he should have taken with him, and linen shirts too fine for battle.

"Be brave, Hope," Father had said when he left.

"I will be most courageous," I replied easily, "as long as I don't have to climb down a ladder, nor up a tree."

He laughed, and so had I. My fear of heights was somewhat of a family joke, except to me. I might laugh about it while safely on the ground, but not when confronted with a climb, up or down. Even our good solid stairs gave me trouble. About other things, say spiders, I was fairly courageous. Now, I was too frightened to be brave, or clever about anything. I only hoped to be quick enough to suit Mr. Thomas.

Shrieks came from downstairs. The men must have found Nan and Martha. Were they being hurt? Would the men respect our serving girls? If only Father, Uncle Seldon, or Peter were here.

The key, tied on a silken cord, turned up in the pocket of Father's waistcoat. I handed it to Mr. Thomas, and he bade us go before him down the stairs.

Mother looked at me with terror in her eyes. "Hope, get the girls."

Mr. Thomas nodded, and I ran into my room. Brewster was filling my pillowcase with our things. I hastened to the bed and scooped up Abigail, and dragged Mary to her feet.

"Stop, Hope, you're hurting," complained Mary.

"Mama!" cried Abigail.

I brought them down the stairs to Mother in the parlor. Mr. Thomas had opened Father's desk and papers were strewn all over the floor. The little girls rushed to Mother and hid in her skirts.

"Where else does Captain Wakeman keep his papers?" demanded Mr. Thomas. "There is nothing of import here."

Mother shook her head. "Only here."

I tried to look as sure as Mother, though I knew Father kept a box for special papers under a loose board where Mr. Thomas was now standing.

Mr. Thomas threw down the drawer he'd been holding, smashing it on the hearth. Mary cried out, and Mother shushed her. Meanwhile, Dimon, in the long dragging coat, was putting everything of value into an old grain sack. He took Father's pen and silver ink pot, wrapped them in one of Grandfather's letters, and tossed them in the sack.

Mr. Thomas herded us through the hall into the lean-to kitchen Father had built only the year before. Nan and Martha were cowering by the hearth while

Percy filled his sack with the fine pewter cups Father had brought from Boston before the massacre at Lexington. Then Percy reached for the dainty English porcelain clock, shaped like a bouquet of flowers, that Grandfather Burr had given Mother as a wedding present. There wasn't another clock like it in Fairfield, perhaps not in all of Connecticut. No one ever touched the clock except Mother, who wound it once every evening after prayers.

"Put that down!" shouted Mother.

Percy looked at her, startled. And for a moment all were silent. Mother stood erect, two red patches of anger on her pale cheeks. "Put it down, sir."

Percy looked from her to Mr. Thomas. Then he wrapped the clock in a dishtowel and put it in his sack.

"Savages!" cried Mother. "Common thieves! Are ye not ashamed?"

"'Tis war, mistress!" said Mr. Thomas.

"'Tis thievery against defenseless women and babes," said Mother.

What made her suddenly so bold? Was she not afraid of what they might do to her? Perhaps she had gone beyond fear. But I had not.

"Ye are dishonest Rebels, enemies of King George. And ye deserve what ill befalls you." Mr. Thomas spoke; the others shuffled their feet and grunted in assent. He took Mother's besom broom, thrust it into the hearth, and pulled out a flaming torch.

"Take this for your sharp tongue and rebel ways!" He threw the burning broom onto Nan's bedstead in the corner.

It took but moments for the fire to catch the bedding. The corn-husk mattress near exploded with flames and sparks. Again, all were held immobile and silent, transfixed by the flames. Mother keened as if she were in pain.

Dimon and Brewster came into the room. Percy grabbed a stick of candlewood, lit it from the hearth, and set fire to the loom and the corner cupboard. Fire crackled and danced maliciously around the room.

"Out, boys," said Mr. Thomas. "Out before we're roasted."

"And them?" Brewster nodded toward us.

"Get them out, too."

We were shoved out the kitchen door, into the sharp November night. We huddled together in the yard, clinging to each other, crying and choking, as thick acrid smoke poured from the house. Mother tucked Jonathan inside her shawl to protect him from the smoke and cold.

The dogs were barking and snapping around the Tories. Jubal sank his teeth into Percy's boot.

"Shoot them!" said Mr. Thomas.

Dimon killed them both with Father's musket. The girls screamed and Mother tried to enfold them in her shift. Then the men set fire to the barn. The milk-cow and sow were turned loose, while the hay, oats, the seed corn for next year, and the plow fed the blaze.

They were taking everything they could carry that was precious, and destroying the rest. Our faithful dogs lay in pools of blood at our feet. And all we could do was watch helplessly and weep. It was unbearable.

Then Mr. Thomas grabbed me and flung me over his shoulder like a sack of corn. I pummeled him with my fists, kicked, and tried to bite him. Although I was nearly thirteen, I was slightly built and no match for someone twice my size, especially as I was hanging upside down.

He turned and spoke to Mother.

"We came for Captain Wakeman but shall take what we can get. Tell your husband he may redeem his daughter from the British garrison at Lloyd's Neck."

Then he strode out of the yard into the darkness.

"No!" Mother cried out. And I raised my head to see her running toward me.

Percy intercepted her and brought his pistol to her head.

"Do not follow," he growled.

The girls wailed. Abigail, Mary, Nan, and Martha caught up with Mother and clung to her. The Tories shouldered their sacks of loot and set off down the path.

"Hope!" cried Mother. "Lord, *help us!*"

The men marched past our gate, across the fields, and down the lane to the river. I was bounced along like the sacks. No matter how I fought, there was no escape from the viselike grip of Mr. Thomas.

I strained to see my family. They were an ever diminishing blur of white between the burning house and barn. Soon I could see nothing through my tear-filled eyes.

"Hope!" Mother's anguished cry traveled across the field, faint and wretched, and was soon swallowed up in the night and lost to me.

2
An Ill Wind

I was pitched into a small open boat, a two-masted shallop, tied up at our dock. The boat stank of rotten fish; it was leaky, too. While the men made preparations to sail, I looked for some chance to escape, but Percy kept his pistol out and his eye on me. I tucked my feet up under me to keep them out of the numbing bilge water, and worried. These men had left my poor sick mother and a newborn babe out in the cold night. What might they do to me?

Brewster had boarded our little dory, the *Liberty*, and was readying it to cast off.

"Lively, lads!" said Mr. Thomas. "And we shall make a good run out with the tide."

"Aye, Mr. Thomas, she's ebbing fast enough," said Dimon.

The men hastily stowed their pillage and freed the shallop. Soon we were sailing swiftly down the Mill River. I was being pulled away from all I held dear. The familiar fields and houses of my neighbors were as fleeting shadows. Far behind them, was the glow and smoke of my home, burning to ashes.

Mr. Thomas had said Father could ransom me from Long Island, but it might be some time before Father would even know what had happened. We spoke the truth when we told the Tories we didn't know Father's whereabouts. What would they do with me on Long Island until I could be redeemed? Officers who were abducted were said to be treated well, but I'd never heard of a girl being taken. What if the British decided I wasn't worth keeping? Nor worth returning? It was said that common soldiers of the Continental army sickened and starved in the Sugar House prison in New York. Would I be sent to die in a moldy prison?

After a while we drew near Perry's mill, home of my best friend, Prudence. The house was right next to the mill on the riverbank. Prudence slept at the back of the house, where a small window faced the river. There was a slight chance that I could rouse her. I leaned as far out from the boat as I dared, and shouted with every ounce of my being, *"Prudence! Hel —"*

My cry was stifled by Mr. Thomas, whose one heavy hand covered my mouth while his other near strangled me.

"If you make another sound," he growled, "he will silence ye!" He nodded toward Percy, who had his pistol trained on me. "Do you understand?"

I nodded as best I could, and he released me. I slumped down in the boat, swallowed up in gloom. Now I felt doubly the cold, damp night, the winds rising off the river, and the complete inadequacy of my shift. I tried to pull some briny sailcloth around me. But mostly I shivered and wept, unaware of anything but my own misery.

The shallop continued rapidly downriver, taking me ever farther from my family. On either bank were friends who would have come to my aid if only they'd known my need. Perhaps Mother had sent Nan to the Perrys' house. . . . Then I remembered, Prudence's father was also gone to fight the British. But perhaps Nan or Martha could find someone else able to rescue me. I tried to think of something, of some way this night might end more happily, but there was *nothing*.

Before long we'd cleared the mouth of the river and proceeded apace into the Sound. There was a heavy salt smell in the air and the cold grew more piercing as we left the shelter of land. And then the wind died! The pull of the tide alone wasn't enough to move the boats. The *Liberty* drew alongside and the men talked. They spoke softly, but I caught the worry in their voices and sat up to hear them better.

"The wind is down for sure," said Percy.

"We are dying in the water," said Brewster, eyeing the limp sails of both boats.

"We'll never make the broad reach across to Oyster Bay!" said Dimon.

I wondered that the boat wasn't going straight to the British at Lloyd's Neck. I didn't know the Long Island towns. Perhaps Lloyd's Neck was part of Oyster Bay, as Southport was part of Fairfield.

"Brewster, are there oars aboard the dory?" asked Mr. Thomas.

"Aye," said Brewster.

The *Liberty* was always fitted out. Pity. I'd rather see her cut adrift than in the hands of Tories.

"Well, use them," said Mr. Thomas. "If we cannot stand out from Fairfield, we'll pull our way across the Sound."

Percy and Mr. Thomas were competent and vigorous at the oars, but Dimon was completely inept. In any event, the shallop was heavy in the water, and they made little gain. I began to feel a glimmer of hope. At this rate the Tories might still be in Fairfield waters when dawn broke. Every moment of their delay meant a chance that Mother would find some means to save me. I said every prayer I could think of to make morning come before my captors could row across the Sound. Even if Nan wasn't able to raise a rescue party, any number of vessels put out to sea each morning. The

Sherwoods' or the Palmers' ketch might be abroad. Surely they would take notice of an unfamiliar boat and the *Liberty* manned by a stranger. What little progress the shallop made, Brewster in the dory made even less. The more the men tired, the slower we went, the more my heart danced.

At length Mr. Thomas called a halt. The men hung over their oars, gulping air. The sails still sagged.

"Percy," said Mr. Thomas. "Didn't your missus send you off with a jug of cider and a meat pie?"

"Aye," said Percy.

"Well, now is the moment to share it out."

"I could do with a drop," called Brewster.

Percy left off his oar and went rummaging in a satchel at the stern of the boat, near where I was sitting.

"Give the girl a pull," said Mr. Thomas.

Percy balked.

"Well, look at her, man," said Mr. Thomas. "She's blue with cold. A sick girl isn't worth much, and a dead one, nothing at all."

Percy handed me the jug, which my frozen hands could barely grasp. I had become so intent on trying to calculate the men's lack of progress that I'd been able to forget, for the moment, the cold. The cider slid down my throat, bringing a flush of warmth. I passed the jug back to Percy.

"Give her your coat, Dimon."

"Why me?" complained Dimon.

"Because the coat hinders your rowing," said Mr. Thomas. "Now give it her!"

"Aye," said Dimon, and reluctantly he undid the buttons and threw the coat at me.

If I weren't so miserably cold, I'd have been loath to touch the filthy thing. No doubt it was also crawling with vermin. But I put it on quick enough. My fingers were too numb to work the buttons. I drew the coat around me like a tent. The cider and the coat made me feel better. But the luffing sails were my true comfort. In them I saw my freedom.

The men ate and drank quickly, then renewed their efforts. The shallop labored in the water while I watched the eastern sky for any hint of sunrise. It may have been my desperate need, but it seemed that there was a faint lightening in the east. As the men strained with all their might to bring us to Long Island, I was trying with all my heart to hang on to the Connecticut shore. While this silent struggle continued, and when it seemed that my prayers might keep us in Fairfield's waters, a fresh breeze came up from the northwest — an ill wind.

"Hurrah!" shouted the men aboard the shallop.

"Hurrah!" echoed Brewster from the *Liberty.*

The sails billowed out. Mr. Thomas quickly traded his oar for the tiller. We were soon skimming along the water, headed for Oyster Bay. And all my hopes were ended.

3

Oyster Bay

The rest of the trip across the Sound was lost to me. I wrapped myself in Dimon's stinking coat and wept an ocean of tears. But once I chanced to look up and catch the eye of Mr. Thomas. His face wore a mixture of pity and scorn. That look dried my eyes. I vowed that from that moment on I would keep my fears and sorrows to myself. The weeping might go on in my heart, but I wouldn't let the Tories see it.

We landed at sunrise. I was dragged from the boat and left to stand on the muddy bank while the men parleyed. I was surprised not to see any sign of the British garrison. If the British had sent these men to capture Father, then wouldn't they have to report back to the British commander? But there was no mention of the British, nor me, only much squabbling over the stolen goods. Mr. Thomas claimed the lion's share, taking all the pewter and silver, saying:

"Was it not my boat that carried you across the Sound? And did you not come away with a tight little dory as ample payment for your trouble? Furthermore, you can each bring some gewgaws home. Won't that please the missus, Percy?"

"The missus will be more interested in a share of the ransom," said Percy.

"Aye," said Brewster. "What about the ransom?"

"That may take some time," said Mr. Thomas, "but you'll each get your share."

"You're a slow man to act," said Brewster. "If we'd gone to Fairfield when we were meant to, we'd have caught the fox in his den. Don't be overlong about arranging the ransom."

"Aye," said Percy.

"Not to worry, my boys," said Mr. Thomas.

The men looked doubtful. Mr. Thomas might have been their leader, but they didn't seem to trust him. And neither would I.

In the end, Mr. Thomas gave them each one of our pewter mugs and their pick of the "gewgaws." But I couldn't watch as they divided up the rest of my family's possessions. At least, I could not watch and keep my resolve not to weep.

When all was shared out as suited Mr. Thomas, Dimon took back his coat. I suppose it was less cold than it had been on the water, but I was so numb and wretched, it felt worse. Mr. Thomas pulled me up a rough path in one direction. The rest went off on another path. Mr. Thomas looked slightly more a gentleman than the other raiders, and being the leader he was the one most likely to take charge of me. But I didn't like going off alone with him. I had no love for the British, although it seemed I would be safer in the hands of soldiers who followed orders, rather than left to one man's whims. Not that I could do anything but stumble along after him. There was no place for me to run to, even if I could run — my legs were so stiff and my feet were frozen. I had to follow along and hope that we would be soon at the garrison, and that the British would treat me civilly.

We crossed a small field and came to an ugly little shack with shutters hanging crookedly. Two large black hounds ran across the dirty yard to us. They snarled and growled at me, looking as if they could and would rip out my throat. Mr. Thomas laughed as I shied away from them.

"Good dogs!" he said. "Let her be."

Then they ignored me and danced around Mr. Thomas, wagging their tails, just as my sweet Jubal and Jack would have greeted Father. Mr. Thomas put down his sack, patted the dogs, and called out to the house.

"Elspeth! Come, wife, see what I've brought you."

He'd brought me to his home, not to the British. What did he mean to do? I had to hope that this was only a short stop on our way to the garrison.

A woman came to the door in her shift, her golden hair loose and curling about her pretty face. Wrapped around her was a large woolen shawl, as red as a love apple.

"So you're back," she said. There wasn't anything in her voice to show she was the least bit pleased.

"What's that?" She pointed to me.

"Treasure," he said, grinning.

Elspeth gave him a sour look.

"You've brought another mouth to feed? You've come with another child for me to care for, when day and night I'm taken up with the babe!"

"The girl will be a help to you," he said, his voice gone as harsh as hers.

Did he mean me to be their servant? Why didn't he say anything to her about the ransom?

"You brought a child in her shift! And I suppose you expect me to provide for her from *my* clothespress!"

Elspeth turned abruptly, went into the house, and slammed the door behind her.

Mr. Thomas glared at the door, but made no move to follow her. Perhaps now he would take me to the British. Though I would have welcomed a warm moment by the hearth.

Moments later the door opened and an old woman, terribly crooked and bent, but neatly dressed, came toward us.

"Son," she said, "what have ye been doing out the whole night long?" Not waiting for a reply, she turned to me. "But what mischief is this? What are you doing with this poor child, nearly naked and mostly frozen?"

She pulled off her soft gray shawl and wrapped it around me. "Come, my dear, we must warm you up first. Later, I will get some answers." She cast a hard look at Mr. Thomas as she brought me inside the house.

She sat me at a rough-hewn bench beside the hearth.

"Hot milk and porridge for you, dear. What is your name?"

"Hope Wakeman," I said through chattering teeth.

"Call me Mother Thomas," she said. She patted my back, then busied herself preparing the porridge.

I had time to look around the mean one-room house. All was dirt and disorder. The bedstead was a tangle of gray linens and quilts. The walls were grimy and the floor unswept. It seemed that the house itself was as foul-tempered as its mistress, who sat opposite me, fiercely rocking a squalling baby. Mr. Thomas came and sat on the other side of the hearth, near his wife.

"I'll have cider with a dram of rum in it, Mother," he said.

"I daresay you will," said Mother Thomas. As bent

as she was, Mother Thomas managed to swing the heavy kettle over the fire.

I was in this miserable place and my beautiful home was a charred ruin. Try as I might, I could make no sense of it.

By and by the porridge and cider were ready; the baby was settled into a fretful sleep. Elspeth put him in a cradle by the bed and came to sit beside her husband. She accepted a bowl of porridge from Mother Thomas with barely a nod.

"So, where did you find this poor child, Son?" asked the old woman.

"She's from Fairfield town," said Mr. Thomas.

"That's not nearby," said his mother.

Elspeth snickered.

"It's across the Sound, in Connecticut," said Mr. Thomas, frowning at his wife.

"But how came she here?"

"I brought her," said Mr. Thomas.

Mother Thomas looked from her son to me, her brow creased. She couldn't have known anything about the raid. And even now with all its evidence before her, she didn't seem to guess what had happened.

"What's in the bag?" asked Elspeth, kicking it with her toe.

"Nothing for an ungrateful wife," said Mr. Thomas, his tone teasing rather than angry.

Elspeth smiled up at him, her rosy cheeks dimpling. "I'm sure I'll be most grateful," she said.

"Then look for yourself."

Elspeth sank to the floor, opened the sack, and greedily began pulling out our things; pewter cups and mugs, silver teaspoons, Jonathan's porringer, given him only last week by Grandmother Burr.

"Now this is what *I* call treasure," she said, her eyes sparkling. She held up Mother's beautiful little clock.

Until then I had been keeping still, trying not to show my distress in any manner. But seeing Jonathan's porringer and Mother's clock undid me. I stood up quickly to keep myself from crying out. The wooden bowl of milk and porridge splattered onto the floor.

"Clumsy girl!" said Elspeth. "You'll get no more porridge."

Mother Thomas looked at me, and I felt she saw the tears I was forcing back. She turned to her son.

"What *is* all this?" Her gentle voice rose in anger.

"Noah sailed across to Fairfield and raided a Rebel's nest," said Elspeth. "Ooh! Look at *this*." She held up Mother's silver teapot.

"Is this true, Son?"

"Aye," said Mr. Thomas without meeting his mother's gaze.

"You stole these things? You *stole* this child?"

"It is war, Mother," he said gruffly.

"It is villainy!" said Mother Thomas. She drew me close. "I wish I had not lived so long to see such shameful doings." She spoke in my ear, but loud enough for all to hear.

"Nonsense!" said Elspeth, tossing her curls. "Noah is merely looking out for his family while he serves King George. But I thought he was bringing back Captain Wakeman."

"Well, the captain wasn't available," said Mr. Thomas. "So I brought back the captain's daughter."

"Oh, Noah, you are an idiot," said Elspeth. "The colonel at Lloyd's Neck won't want a *girl*. They could exchange Captain Wakeman for one of the captured British officers. But a girl isn't even worth one of the Hessian soldiers!"

"She's worth something to her family," said Mr. Thomas.

Elspeth snorted. Mother Thomas hugged me tightly.

"This is evil talk," she said. "Think how it would be if Hope's friends or relations came raiding Oyster Bay!"

"That's enough!" said Mr. Thomas. "There'll be no more talk on it."

There followed an uneasy silence. Elspeth returned to unloading the sack and gloating over its contents. She cooed over Mother's fine brass candlesticks, and was moved to jump up and kiss her husband when she uncovered the large silver salver that Martha kept polished as bright as a pier glass.

Mother Thomas had fetched me more porridge and gently encouraged me to eat. But my hunger was gone. At length she drew me up, saying, "Come, child, let us see if we can dress you decently."

She led me to a rickety ladder I'd had my back to and not noticed until now. It went up to an attic loft. I stopped dead at the ladder. I can't, I thought. I can't go up, and then go *down* again later.

"What is the matter, Hope?" Mother Thomas asked.

Fortunately Elspeth and Mr. Thomas were too busy sorting through the stolen loot to pay any attention to us.

"I'm afraid of heights," I whispered.

"Oh."

She didn't laugh at me, nor brush aside my fears as strangers often did. She looked around the room; so did I. There was a bed built into one corner for Mr. Thomas and Elspeth, the cradle for the babe, and nothing else. There was nowhere for me to sleep, nowhere to be away from Elspeth and Mr. Thomas. And I wanted to get as far from them as possible.

"I'll go up," I whispered, and clutched the ladder.

"Close your eyes," said Mother Thomas. "I'll tell you when to open them. I'll be right behind you, Hope. You won't fall."

I nodded, but my stomach turned as rung after rung I crawled up to the loft.

When Mother Thomas told me to open my eyes, I tried to convince myself that I was *not* standing at the top of an old, about-to-split-in-many-pieces ladder, but merely a step below the loft. I heaved myself onto the loft floor, immediately rolled away from the opening, and lay panting on my side. Mother Thomas came quickly after me.

"Well done," she said, and patted my hand. I stayed hugging the floor until the waves of nausea ebbed. Most of the room was taken up with the autumn harvest. A corn-husk mattress made up tidily with a pieced quilt occupied the corner near the chimney. On the wall nearby were shelves edged with paper lace, holding a few precious possessions. Next to the shelves was a row of pegs, where hung a few suits of clothes. Everything was old and simple, but of finer stuff than I would have expected to find in such a mean little house.

"I am ashamed to have you see how I live," said Mother Thomas. "From your family's possessions I can tell you're used to better." Mother Thomas looked around her attic and sighed. "I was used to better, as well. I've not much to offer you, but I can see that you're properly covered." She opened a trunk and began pulling out linens and dark woolen garments to clothe me. I watched her, feeling tired and dazed. I was glad to be away from Elspeth and Mr. Thomas, to be spared the sight of Elspeth pawing my mother's things. It still seemed impossible that this was happening, that Elspeth held the delicate bouquet of Mother's clock, while Mother held ashes and I was in this strange attic.

It didn't seem as if Mr. Thomas had any intention of delivering me to the British anytime soon. I would be completely at his mercy, and that of Elspeth. It was not a hopeful picture. I had to think of some way to get away from them, perhaps get to the British on my own. How could I be ransomed if no one knew where I was?

Mother Thomas was all kindness and concern as she bustled around me, holding up items of clothing to see what would best suit me. I felt she was trying to make up for the cruelty and indifference of her son and Elspeth. Yet, she must have been a Loyalist, too.

I was fitted out with a bodice, petticoat, skirt, stockings, and sleeves. The clothes were old and patched in places, but of good cloth, well made, and still quite respectable.

"There was a time I'd have had more than these few rags to dress you in," said Mother Thomas. "And my clothes have held up better than my shoes. I've nothing for your feet but these old slippers."

Old indeed. They were satin slippers meant for a ball long ago. Now they were more holes than slipper. We would have been ashamed for Nan or Martha to have to wear such ruined things. And, worse, the slippers were far too big for me, and there was no way to secure them.

"Perhaps Elspeth will lend you her boots to get about with," said Mother Thomas. "Or we can share my old boots."

I didn't think Elspeth was very likely to lend me anything, but I kept my thoughts to myself.

As small and bent as she was, Mother Thomas's clothes hung hugely upon me. She got out her scissors, needle, and thread, and with her crippled hands, she helped me remake her well-worn clothes. She was as kind to me as my own Grandmother Burr. But even this old woman's kindness was unbearable. She wasn't my grandmother; she was a stranger, and I didn't want her kindness, or her sad, old clothes. I wanted to be in my own home with my family, where I belonged. I wanted my own clothes, I wanted to be waking up in bed with my two little sisters. I had nothing to do with this war. Wasn't it bad enough that Father was on the battlefield? Why should Mother, baby Jonathan, and the girls have to suffer? Where was Mother now? Was she all right? Why oh why was I here? Oh, how I wanted my mother.

4
Slavey

Two weeks went by, two long weeks. Mr. Thomas kept putting off going to the British, despite Elspeth's constant nagging to "get on with it." So I never knew from day to day what would become of me. But the worst was not knowing what had happened to my family. I was stuck with that awful picture of them out in the cold night between the burning house and burning barn. I did my best to construct a reasonable and hopeful story of what might have happened next. Mother would have sent Nan to get help from the Perrys. Mrs. Perry would have quickly sent her wagon, laden with quilts, to fetch them. Pru would have helped her mother care for them all, fixing up beds and making hot drinks. The next day word would have been sent to Grandmother Burr in Litchfield. Grandfather Wakeman in Stratford was closer, but his house was small and Mother would want to be with her own mother. Grandmother Burr would come immediately to help nurse Mother and Jonathan. When they were well enough she'd carry them all safely to her home.

I couldn't know if any of this was true, though I tried hard to believe in it. During the day I succeeded, but at night I was plagued with that last terrible image of them. I'd be abed wide awake and worrying, although keeping still so as not to disturb Mother Thomas. But she knew I was troubled without my saying a word. She'd rub my back and soothe me to sleep, saying, "Don't fret. Don't fret. All will come right. You'll see, all will be well."

Finally Mr. Thomas announced that he was going to the British garrison at Lloyd's Neck.

"Now don't go blurting out *everything*," said Elspeth. "The British colonel mightn't take kindly to kidnapping. Find out first if the girl is worth anything to the British."

"I've made my strike against the Rebels," said Mr. Thomas. "No doubt, I'll get a reward from the British as well as the ransom."

"Hmph!" said Elspeth. "At least remember to get me some sewing silk from town."

As soon as Mr. Thomas was out the door, she started.

"You stupid girl! There you are lazing about when there is a burden of work to be done." And then she pinched me. Whenever Mr. Thomas wasn't around to see, she was likely to pinch or slap me. But no matter what she said or did, I kept my vow and never cried out or shed a tear that she could see.

"Elspeth!" said Mother Thomas. "There's no call for that. Hope is helping me with these apples."

We'd been paring and stringing apples to dry since before daybreak.

"Well, I need her to wash the baby's linens. Girl, fetch water to fill the wash kettle."

"That is too heavy a task for Hope," said Mother Thomas. "Noah will fill the kettle when he returns."

Elspeth flew at Mother Thomas in such a rage she looked ready to strike her.

"The girl will do whatever I tell her," said Elspeth. "This is my house, and she is mine to command. Don't interfere, old woman. And don't be carrying tales to Noah, for he won't hear you!"

Mother Thomas stood as tall as she could, glaring at Elspeth. But she held her tongue. There was no reasoning with Elspeth. It only made her rage the more. I'd never before seen anyone so full of fury. She pretended to defer to Mr. Thomas, but in fact, she ruled the house. With Mr. Thomas she mostly used sweet words and dimples to get her way. To Mother Thomas and myself, she did nothing to disguise her foul temper. Mother Thomas said it was because Elspeth had thought she was marrying up, but Mr. Thomas had been a big disappointment, having lost all the money he'd inherited. I thought Elspeth was simply mean.

Mother Thomas picked up the buckets and led the way out of the house with dignity. I followed quickly behind, glad to get outside, away from Elspeth, and where I might have a private word with Mother Thomas.

When we were far enough from the house, I spoke. "Do you think Mr. Thomas is arranging for my ransoming today?"

"I believe that is his intent," said Mother Thomas.

"But why didn't he take me with him?"

"Elspeth wouldn't let him," said Mother Thomas. "She may be right that the British officers will not condone common kidnapping."

"Then what will happen to me?"

Mother Thomas couldn't answer me, nor meet my eye. They would keep me here to be Elspeth's slave.

"I can't stay here," I said. "I must get back. Mother must be so worried, and she needs me more than ever. And I . . ."

"I promise I will find a way to help you," said Mother Thomas. "But surely the British officers will take an interest in your case and arrange for your safe return to your family in Connecticut."

Elspeth opened the door and shouted, "Stop your nattering!"

"Don't despair," whispered Mother Thomas as she handed me a full bucket of water.

I tried to smile. "All right," I said.

Struggling to and from the house with the heavy buckets, I tried to set my mind at rest. I wanted to believe that the British would help me. Mother had always maintained that the British officers were gentlemen — unlike Mr. Thomas and his fellow raiders. But would they do the gentlemanly thing and arrange for my redemption and quick return? If Father couldn't be notified, I knew Grandmother Burr would find whatever money was necessary to ransom me. Even if they were the enemy, I didn't think the British would use me as badly as Elspeth did. After all, I was a prisoner of war, not a slavey. But perhaps a girl couldn't be a prisoner of war. Perhaps the British would give me to the Hessian mercenaries. I'd heard Nan tell Martha, when she thought I wasn't listening, that the Hessians did unspeakable things to girls. I wasn't too sure what she meant, but I certainly didn't want to find out.

"You are slower than snails," said Elspeth. "There is so much to be done. Here I am left with a fretful babe, an old, crippled woman, and a useless girl, while my husband is gadding about."

Even though we had lived in a fine house and had servants, I was no stranger to work. I had always helped Mother, Martha, and Nan. We had a pump right inside our kitchen, and for heavy tasks, such as rendering fat for candles and soap, or washday, Peter had helped in the kitchen or Father hired Mrs. Squire and her niece to help. I didn't mind most of the tasks Elspeth set me, except that she had an uncanny way of demanding things that required climbing up and down the ladder, or standing on the stool. She kept sending me up to the attic to fetch an onion or dried corn, or she'd have me sweeping cobwebs from the ceiling, or picking apples. I tried not to let her see how much heights bothered me, knowing she'd find a way to make it worse.

The work kept me busy, although I couldn't leave off worrying about my family for long. Once they got to Grandmother Burr's in Litchfield, I knew they'd be safe. But what if Mother had caught a chill that terrible night of the raid? She was already so weak from Jonathan's birth. And Jonathan was so tiny and fragile. Even a short time out in the cold night without shelter might have harmed him greatly. And what of Abigail and Mary? They were still so little. How had they fared? I went over it again and again, hoping the best for all of them, fearing the worst, and unable to know anything.

I minded that and Elspeth's ordering me about, insisting that *I* was a slow-witted, slothful creature, when in fact she was too indolent to bother to dress herself properly. She spent most of her day in her shift, with the red shawl slipping off her shoulders, complaining about her hard life. And, as much as anything, I minded how badly she treated Mother Thomas. It was shameful.

By late afternoon Mr. Thomas still hadn't returned, and Elspeth was afire, crackling with nerves and irritation. She handed me a basket and pointed to the orchard.

Lord help me, I thought, not the apples again! I'd been picking apples with Mr. Thomas for the past three days. It had been a trial I thought was behind me.

"Get the last of the apples," said Elspeth. "And don't try going beyond the orchard or the dogs will bring you back in pieces."

The dogs had been trained to keep all strangers off the cleared land surrounding the house. Likewise, they knew to keep the pig, sheep, and hens from straying. My first day in Oyster Bay, Mr. Thomas had trained them to treat me like one of the sheep.

"It's too late in the day," said Mother Thomas. "She'll take a chill."

"She'll do no such thing," said Elspeth. "Tonight there may be a hard frost. I want every apple we can get off those trees."

"There aren't any good apples left to be picked," I said, for once speaking up.

"None of your sass," said Elspeth, slapping me. "Don't come back 'til you fill the basket."

The only apples left on the trees were too worm-eaten to be worth picking. But Elspeth seemed intent on getting me out of the house, as if she could no longer bear the sight of me. I couldn't know what went on in her mind, but I felt that she increasingly rued my presence. Taking me had been a mistake for which she blamed me as much as Mr. Thomas.

Mother Thomas followed after me, wrapping her heavy shawl around my shoulders.

"Likely you'll fill the basket soon enough," she said. "But come back before then if you get too cold."

"Or if I fall out of a tree," I said.

"You needn't do any climbing," she said, and winked.

She was right. With no one watching over me, I could fill the basket with the rotting windfalls. I smiled. "Would the dogs really hunt me down?" I asked.

"They're quite fierce and they know you are not to leave the farm," said Mother Thomas. "Hope, don't think of running away. Where could you go? It's much too dangerous, and with no shoes and winter coming on."

I could go to the garrison, I thought, if only I knew the way to Lloyd's Neck. Perhaps I could follow along the shore until I found a boat to steal, and sail home. But I couldn't sail the smallest craft on my own, and certainly not across the Sound. Nor could I walk around the Sound to Connecticut in November, not even in summer, as Mother Thomas pointed out, without shoes upon my feet.

When I got to the orchard, I climbed the little hill and looked beyond the trees, over the cove to the Sound. Home was so close — so far away. I picked up the wormy apples and tried to think of some way to get home. My hands and feet grew numb with the cold. There might indeed be a frost. If only I had shoes, my own soft brown leather boots; I could walk home. If only I knew the way. If only I . . .

The dogs watched my every move. When I got to the tree at the far end of the orchard, I tried ambling my way to the stand of pines, just to see what would happen. Sure enough, the dogs were there before me, barring my way, teeth bared and growling.

"G-g-good dogs," I said. "Good dogs." And I headed quickly back to the apple trees and carried on.

When the basket was nearly full I stopped and looked again to the Sound, which stretched out all the way to the Connecticut shore. Evening had come on, and the sky was so clear that far across the water I could see the winking gleam of a lighthouse. It might have been Fairfield's lighthouse at Black Rock. My home, I thought, my lost home. If only I could send a message. Put a letter in a bottle and cast it across the water. Or simply speak to them.

"Mother," I said softly. *"Mother! Father! Help me!"* I called with all my heart. The wind off the water blew the words back to me, and the awful black dogs began to bark.

I lugged the basket back to the house, wanting news of Mr. Thomas as much as the hearth.

But when I got back, with the moon already high in the sky, Mr. Thomas hadn't yet returned. Elspeth was in a fearful temper. She kicked me, shoved Mother Thomas, and once nearly struck Nathan, her own little son. But Mother Thomas scooped up the crying babe before Elspeth could harm him, and rocked him safely to sleep.

During our supper of corn mush with stewed currants, Elspeth could hardly sit still. She was constantly at the window, looking for signs of her husband, muttering, "The fool, the foolish man, with all his swaggering and bragging, the British will have thrown him into their stinking prison. Isn't my life hard enough? Oh, the *fool!*"

Neither Mother Thomas nor I spoke. Mother Thomas seemed worried about her son. Although it grieved her, I was glad to think of Mr. Thomas imprisoned.

When the dishes were washed, the pots scoured, and the fire banked, Mother Thomas and I climbed the ladder to the loft. I wouldn't go up to the loft unless Mother Thomas was behind me, guiding my feet and whispering encouragement. Once in bed, I couldn't sleep in spite of my weariness. I kept thinking that a parade of Redcoats would come marching up to the house. I knew it was stupid to think the enemy would rescue me, but I was that needful.

Deep in the middle of the night, the door burst open. I sat up, my heart thumping. Was this my salvation? I crept nearer to the loft opening and dared to peer into the dimness below.

It was Mr. Thomas, alone. And from the fumes that drifted into the attic, he was much the worse for drink.

"You were right, wife," he shouted, stumbling around the room, as cumbersome as a bear. "The Redcoats didn't want to hear about the girl. They told me to take her back! HA!"

"Hush!" said Elspeth. "You drunken sot, you'll wake the baby."

He'd already woken Mother Thomas, who was sitting up in bed, her mobcap slightly askew. For a moment I dared hope that Mr. Thomas would take me home.

"It'll be a cold day in hell before I risk my neck again in Rebel waters, and for the sake of a girl! HA!"

"Oh, do shut up, Noah," said Elspeth. "I must think."

"A man goes out and risks his neck for his king, and what thanks does he get?" Mr. Thomas sank down on the bench by the hearth. "Nothing!"

"We'll have to get rid of her," said Elspeth.

"Absolutely nothing," mourned Mr. Thomas.

Get rid of me. What was she saying?

"Hope," whispered Mother Thomas. She'd brought the quilt, and sat beside me, wrapping us both in its warmth. No matter the quilt, I couldn't stop shaking.

"You can carry the girl to New York in the shallop and sell her to one of the fine houses," said Elspeth.

Mr. Thomas moaned, then belched. I bit my hand to keep from screaming.

There was a moment of silence below, and I could just feel Elspeth wondering if she ought to climb the ladder to check if we were still asleep, but she made not a move. When she spoke again her voice was pitched so low I had to crane forward to hear her.

"Better yet, we'll let the Hunting Town trader handle it. He'll take her where questions won't be asked."

"Nothing," sighed Mr. Thomas. "Absolutely nothing."

A slave trader! They'd sell me into servitude just like that! *No*, I thought, this is *not* happening. I cannot, I will not let it happen. I wouldn't let them trade me like baggage. I'd run away in my shift if I had to. I'd not be sold!

5

Escape

"Come, my dear," said Mother Thomas, drawing me away from the opening. "We've heard enough."

We climbed back into our bed, and unable to stop myself, I burst into tears.

"Hush, child, hush," murmured Mother Thomas. "Don't let them hear you."

But fear and grief tore out of me in great wrenching sobs. Mother Thomas held me to her breast, patting my back as I'd often seen her do to soothe the babe. And, bit by bit, I too was soothed.

Fortunately, Mr. Thomas continued to make such a noise below that it would have been nearly impossible for Elspeth to hear me.

When I had calmed down, Mother Thomas held me at arm's length and whispered fiercely, "None of what she's said will happen, Hope. We'll leave here together."

I couldn't understand what she was saying.

"*I* will take you to your home," she said.

I stared at her in the darkness. There was just enough moonlight to see that she was serious. This Tory woman, whom I'd only known for two weeks, was not only going to help me escape, she was going to take me herself!

I hugged Mother Thomas and cried a flood of silent tears, the overflow of my brimming heart.

Over the next several days and nights, as we prepared to leave, I worried about Mother Thomas. She seemed too old and frail to embark on such an adventure. Yet she was intent on going. I wanted to leave at once, but Mother Thomas felt we should look the part of traveling ladies, not runaways. I argued with her late at night in whispers. I feared the sudden arrival of the Hunting Town trader. Mother Thomas assured me that that was impossible, and insisted on careful preparations.

"Best we appear as well-to-do as possible," said Mother Thomas. "We'll need plenty of help, and no one wants to help beggars."

So we turned and altered a suit of fine black bombazine to fit me neatly. Mother Thomas made over bonnets for us both in the new style. Elspeth interrupted our preparations with her frequent demands. But Elspeth was so lazy even her vigilance was lax. She'd set me a task, then often fall into a doze with the napping baby.

Late at night, when we were sure Elspeth and Mr. Thomas slept, we talked. Mother Thomas said she had a friend in Bayville, not too far from here. And this friend, Pruitt Jones, had a boat, a Long Island coaster.

"He'll take us to Fairfield?" I couldn't believe it would be so easy.

"No," said Mother Thomas.

"Oh."

"He'd never sail in Rebel waters," she said, "and I'll not ask him to take that risk. I don't want Pruitt Jones to know anything about you, or to be involved in our scheme."

"But . . ."

"As you know, Elspeth has quite a temper. She also has two nasty-minded brothers. If she thinks Pruitt Jones has helped us, she'll get her brothers to do him harm. Pruitt often goes to New York, trading this and that. He'll take us there, and no one will think anything of his going."

New York wouldn't have been my first choice. The British had beaten General Washington there at the beginning of the war, and had kept control of the town. The British soldiers were there in force, and Loyalists from all over the country had flocked there. Father said that nearly half the city burned down right after the British took possession. What was left of the town was terribly crowded. Many of the public buildings had been turned into prisons for Rebels and captured soldiers of the Continental army. Going to New York felt as if I'd be trading the frying pan for the fire.

"Don't worry, my dear," said Mother Thomas. "I'm quite confident travel from New York to Bedford, near Connecticut, can be easily arranged. My mother's family was from those parts. Once we get there, my cousins will see you the rest of the way home."

"Will your cousins want to help a Rebel?"

"My cousins may be loyal to King George, but that won't keep them from doing right by you. We are an honorable family, and there is nothing honorable in kidnapping!"

"What will you do after Bedford?" I asked.

"I shall stay on. I'm done with Oyster Bay."

I was glad for her to be getting away from Elspeth's temper and her son's indifference. Then I thought of her rocking the babe, smoothing his wraps and stroking his soft cheeks. It would be a sad parting for her.

"What if you'd just help me get started?" I asked. "I could go on my own once I was set on the right path."

"No," whispered Mother Thomas. "There are far too many dangers for a young girl on her own. Besides, I cannot stay here. You've seen how I'm treated. I've some silver put by, and a few trinkets. I shall use them to see some peace at the end of my days."

"When was the last time you saw your Bedford cousins?" I asked.

"It's been a few years," she said, "though we write often. I imagine they are quite old, and gray now, too." Mother Thomas smoothed her hair and sniffed. "No more questions for now, Hope. Go to sleep."

I closed my eyes, but sleep wouldn't come. I wondered if I'd ever sleep again as I had in my own soft bed with my sisters' steady breath stirring the air. Perhaps I'd not sleep well until I was safely with my family. Perhaps not even then.

For now sleep would wait. I'd too much to think about. Mother Thomas was a Tory. By rights she was my enemy. But she had put aside all that to help me.

When Papa had explained the Rebellion to me, it had all been so clear. King George was a tyrant who had denied the Colonists their basic rights. Our war was just. The British were wrong, and the Tories who supported the British were wrong. We *had* to fight against them.

Mother Thomas was as kind as my own Grandmother Burr. I could never call her foe. And I thanked God she was my friend.

Even with Mother Thomas's help I had many worries. What if our plan didn't work? What if we were caught escaping? What if Mr. Thomas and Elspeth remembered the Bedford cousins? Would they track us that far? What would happen to Mother Thomas once we were in Bedford? I couldn't imagine her cousins would be pleased to take in an old woman when they were likely to be feeling the pinched circumstances of the war. Could my family offer her a home, when we no longer had a home of our own? I was so very tired, but all my worries kept sleep at bay.

During the day, the hardest part was pretending that nothing was different, that I didn't know of Elspeth's horrid plan to sell me into servitude, and that I hadn't a plan of my own. Every once in a while I'd catch Elspeth watching me. Did she wonder if I'd heard her plan? I'd try to look engrossed in the task at hand, and sad, as if I were thinking about my family. I *was* thinking about my family, but I wasn't sad now. I was frightened, nervous, and terribly excited. Perhaps in a few days I would be with them again. I might even be in Litchfield in time to celebrate Thanksgiving! The nightmare was coming to an end. I was so stirred up, I could barely keep inside my own skin.

Every time Mr. Thomas walked out the door I was sure he was off to fetch the Hunting Town trader. But he was his usual self, loath to proceed on any new course. Elspeth would prod him daily about going to Hunting Town. She'd look at him and say in a mean-

ingful way, "We ought to get the Hunting Town business settled before the British think to take an interest,
my dear husband."

Then Mr. Thomas would laugh. "Yes, wife, soon
enough. I've one or two more things to take care of
afore I'm off."

I could tell that Elspeth was boiling, but she reined
herself in to reply, "As you will, *husband*."

Mr. Thomas's procrastination gave Mother Thomas
and me enough time to carry on with our preparations.
I was willing to risk looking a bit shabby if it brought
me that much sooner to my mother. But Mother
Thomas insisted that the care we took readying our escape would ensure its success.

Meanwhile, Elspeth seemed to be trying to get as
much work out of me as possible, setting me all
the heavy, dirty tasks she could think of. I scoured
the floor with salt, beat the braided rugs, and washed
the bed covers, the linens, the baby's clouts, and shirts,
shifts, gowns, and petticoats. Aside from all the tasks
that required standing on a stool or ladder, I minded
the washing more than anything else. Especially as
it was clear that Elspeth seldom, if ever, had washed
many of the things she so readily piled up for me
to wash. Every day the sun shone was washday.
Each dawn I prayed fervently for rain. The Thomas's
house was mean and shabby, but with my family's

pewter and silver and my hard work, it had become much nicer.

I told Mother Thomas that I intended to take back my family's stolen possessions.

"I wish I could bring back everything that was stolen, including the *Liberty*." I also wished that I could somehow undo all the work I'd done, and leave Elspeth's home as dirty as I'd found it. But I didn't say that.

"All that will truly matter to your family is that you get back safely," said Mother Thomas. "But it's right that you retrieve as many of your family's things as possible."

So we began to piece together two satchels from some stout sailcloth Mother Thomas found in the shed. Each satchel was lined with pockets to protect the silver and pewter and keep it from clanking. As much as I saw the usefulness of our work, I was maddened by the extra time it took. We agreed to leave behind the large silver salver. It would be too conspicuous to carry about. Mother Thomas said it would be ample payment for Elspeth's boots and shawl, and for what we'd need from the larder. I thought we should take Elspeth's cloak as well, but Mother Thomas said it wouldn't be Christian to leave Elspeth without any protection from the cold. We'd have two warm shawls, and Mother Thomas's old cloak, and that would be enough.

At last we were ready to set out, and truly, I don't think I could have borne another day of waiting. We planned to leave soon after Elspeth and Mr. Thomas had settled in for the night. The baby usually woke in the very early hours for a feeding. We had to hope that when Elspeth nursed him she wouldn't notice anything amiss. We needed as much of an advance as possible. Mother Thomas said her friend was only a few miles away, but I didn't know how long that would take, burdened as we'd be.

We soon heard the rhythmic snoring of Mr. Thomas, which nightly filled the house. It was harder to be sure if Elspeth slept. She might well have been wide awake, reckoning my worth. We waited many heartbeats until we could hear her shallow, even breathing between his snores. When all was still below us, Mother Thomas produced the leather grip she'd packed with what clothes weren't already on our bodies and her few possessions. We took the sailcloth satchels out from under the mattress. Then Mother Thomas made up her bed as neatly as she did each morning, smoothing the patched quilt and patting the pillows.

Mother Thomas went down the ladder first. She moved slowly, the ladder complaining with every step. I couldn't bear to watch. I lay on my stomach near the opening, ready to pass her the bags. That was accomplished easily and silently. Then it was my turn.

I'd learned to descend the ladder keeping most of my weight on my stomach while my feet searched for the first rung, and then slowly lower myself. With my first step the ladder creaked, sounding as loud as a pistol shot. This *would* be the time the rickety thing really did break apart, sending me crashing to the ground. But no, all was well. I made it safely down. Elspeth, Mr. Thomas, and the baby slept on.

While Mother Thomas busied herself in the pantry, I took the satchels and tiptoed around the house, reclaiming our stolen silver and pewter. At any second the baby might cry and ruin my chance of leaving. When I tried to get Jonathan's porringer from the shelf near the baby's cradle, he did whimper. Elspeth stirred in her sleep. I crouched on the floor by the cradle and pleaded silently with the baby, "Please, please sleep on, little baby." But no, he whimpered again. Soon he'd wake Elspeth. My heart beat so, I thought I'd die right then. Instead I reached out and gently rocked the cradle. Nathan found his fist to suck on and was quiet again.

My hands shook as I took Mother's china clock from the shelf above Elspeth's bed. I had to lean over Mr. Thomas to get it. His hot, sour breath rose up to gag me. I was so nervous, what if I dropped the clock on his head? And what would happen should Elspeth and Mr. Thomas catch me? I grasped the precious clock and hugged it to my chest. With careful steps I crossed the room and nodded to Mother Thomas. Then she handed me Elspeth's boots, thick woolen stockings, and Elspeth's pride and joy, her bright red shawl. There were only two more obstacles to our leaving — the dogs! Mother Thomas had a big piece of bacon for them wrapped in a napkin. We'd talked about this, but I remained filled with misgivings.

"Whatever happens," said Mother Thomas, "keep calm, and *don't* run."

Mother Thomas took one last look at Nathan's cradle and sighed. Then we tiptoed out of the house. I carried the satchels and the grip so that Mother Thomas would have her hands free to bribe the dogs. I eased the door shut, grateful that just two days before, Elspeth had made me grease the rusted and squeaking hinges.

The dogs came to us warily with low growls. There was a terrible moment of not knowing what they'd do. Their teeth were bared and they looked ready to lunge at us. I wanted more than anything to run, but forced myself to hold still. At last, they sniffed the small piece of bacon Mother Thomas held out. Their tails began to wag, and they ate. We walked slowly past them, and down the path that led behind the house in a direction unknown to me. A few yards beyond the house, and out of sight of the dogs, Mother Thomas stopped.

"All right?" she asked.

I nodded, though my insides were still quaking.

Mother Thomas wrapped me in the red shawl and fastened it on with Elspeth's own silver brooch. I sat on a stone and, with shaking hands, pulled on the woolen stockings. Mother Thomas handed me bits of rag to stuff in the toes of the boots. When I was done they fit me quite well. While I was tying on my new bonnet, the dogs approached. They circled around us, this time growling in earnest.

"G-g-good dogs," said Mother Thomas, and she fumbled in her pocket.

One bark and Mr. Thomas would waken, and it would be all over.

Mother Thomas pulled out a napkin-wrapped bundle. It was another, larger piece of bacon. The dogs eyed it hungrily.

"Get it," she whispered, and flung the bacon some yards back toward the house. The dogs leapt after it. We picked up our bags and set off briskly.

The night was faintly lit by a quarter moon. We hadn't much time to get away before we would be missed. I knew Elspeth wouldn't let Mr. Thomas rest until he'd retrieved us and the stolen treasure. All was uncertain and full of peril. The ground was rimed with frost, a small sign of the coming winter. It wasn't a good time to be without shelter. But I was wearing Elspeth's sturdy boots and her warm, thick shawl. I wouldn't mind the cold so much. The impossible was happening. Mother Thomas and I were on our way. I was heading back to my family.

6

The Marianne

The path leading away from the Thomases soon became a rough track through a wood. We stopped and
removed our boots and stockings to cross two icy
streams. Come morning, the dogs wouldn't have so easy
a job tracking us. I also hoped that Mr. Thomas would
be, as ever, unable to leap into action. No doubt
Elspeth would goad and push, but perhaps *he* would
take his time coming after us.

I'd never before been out walking at night. Night-
time, decent people were in their beds. Although I was
only taking back myself and what belonged to my family, I felt like a thief. Fear of being caught was just part
of it. I didn't like being out with the wild creatures. I
don't suppose there was anything more dangerous in
the woods than a fox, but my skin prickled and I
jumped at every snapping twig.

It was a relief to get to the cultivated fields of the next farmsteads. But these were, in truth, more dangerous than the wilds. Farms meant dogs. Usually they were tied up at night, but we couldn't be sure. Even a tied dog can bark. We didn't want anyone hereabouts to know of our leaving. So we kept as far from the houses and barns as possible, though it meant stumbling over the stubble of corn fields, tripping over pumpkin vines, and slogging through the muddy furrows. I fell several times, bruising my hands and knees. It was a good thing Mother Thomas was carrying Mother's clock, else I'd be bringing it back in pieces.

Mother Thomas kept up a steady pace, but her face looked strained and her breath was terribly uneven. I pretended fatigue just to make her rest. We sat on a fallen log on a little rise above a corn field. The faint moonlight showed that Long Island farms were like our own in Fairfield. It was strange to think that someplace so familiar was enemy territory. Although there were probably some Patriots in Long Island as there were Loyalists in Connecticut.

"Mother Thomas, why are you a Loyalist?" I asked.

She looked at me, startled.

"Well, England will always be our mother country as King George is our loving father. I don't think there is cause to part from either England or the king."

"That makes me your enemy."

"No, you are like a child of my own."

"But my father would be your enemy."

"Dear me, Hope." Mother Thomas looked perplexed. "I can't agree with the Rebellion. Neither can I think of all revolutionaries as my enemies. Your parents and I might well be friends. We'd better move along, now."

I helped her stand and noticed her wince as she picked up the grip.

"Let me carry it," I said.

"I can manage," she said, and smiled.

I leaned forward and kissed her. She touched my cheek, then we trudged on again. Mother Thomas was, indeed, my friend. Yet Mr. Thomas, her son, had burned down my home. It was a cruel puzzle where the pieces would never properly fit together.

"Is it much further?" I asked, once we'd crossed the next field.

"A few more corn fields and several pastures," said Mother Thomas. "A road will take us part of the way."

A road sounded a good deal easier going than the fields and pastures. At first it was. We walked down the middle where it wasn't so rutted and muddy. We were going along fine, except the straps of the satchels had already raised blisters on my hands. And then I heard the hoofbeats. We hadn't deceived anyone! Mr. Thomas was nearly upon us! I looked to Mother Thomas, too stunned and fearful to move. She pulled me off the road into some briars just as a Redcoat on a huge horse galloped past us.

It wasn't Mr. Thomas. With any luck, he was still abed and snoring. The night rider hadn't seen us, thanks to Mother Thomas and the darkness.

"There probably won't be any other soldiers about," Mother Thomas whispered. "But I'd rather not have to explain myself to anyone. Shall we go back to the fields?"

So we returned to the muddy ground. The satchels grew heavier with every step, but now I was too afraid to rest. If Mr. Thomas had woken and missed us, he *could* come after us as swiftly as the British soldier. I tried to think only of my family. Each step forward was one step closer to them. What joy it would be to see them all again, to find them well and happy. I tried not to think of our house in flames, nor of all my worries for Mother, the girls, and Jonathan. Instead I pictured them happy, well, and holding me in their arms.

Mother Thomas had said that it shouldn't take more than a week or two to get to Fairfield. Two weeks — surely for two weeks I could be patient.

Come dawn we were struggling up a rocky hill toward a ramshackle cottage perched on its crest when Mother Thomas grasped my arm and pulled me to a stop. She was quite pale and breathing so raggedly she couldn't speak.

"Are you all right?" I dropped my burdens to support her.

"I'm . . . I'm . . ." She waved away my arms and finally caught her breath. "I'm fine, but I must warn you about my friend."

I waited for her to continue, wishing we weren't so out in the open.

"I didn't want to tell you before. It would only worry you," said Mother Thomas. "He has no love for the Rebels. I will tell him you are Elspeth's orphaned niece going to other relations in New York. He isn't likely to question you too closely about it. Anyway, don't be alarmed, whatever he says or does. Pruitt Jones is an odd sort, but not dangerous."

How could I pretend to be Elspeth's niece when I knew so little about her, and none of it good? And what did Mother Thomas mean by "odd"?

"Now don't fret," said Mother Thomas, breathing steadily once more. "It will be fine." She brushed the dirt from her skirts, smoothed her silver hair, straightened her bonnet, and picked up the grip. Then she led the way up to the cottage and knocked on the door. I grabbed the satchels and caught up with her.

"Go away!" roared someone from inside.

"Open up, Pruitt," said Mother Thomas. "It's Maude Thomas."

The door opened a crack. "Give me a sign," he said, "that it's really you and not some Rebel come to cut out my heart and eat it for dinner."

"Pruitt, you old codfish," said Mother Thomas. "Don't you recognize me?"

"You've aged," said Pruitt Jones, opening the door two inches more.

"No more than you," said Mother Thomas, and she smiled.

"But you're still a beautiful woman, Maude Thomas," said Pruitt Jones, and he opened the door wide.

There he stood, a tall, skin-and-bones old man. His face was wreathed with wrinkles, and weathered brown as a walnut. Bright, wild blue eyes stared out of that ancient face. His long matted hair and bristling whiskers framed his face in startling white. His clothes hung on him in tatters. And it didn't seem as if Pruitt Jones had ever washed his clothes or himself.

"Where's your horse?" asked Pruitt Jones.

"We walked," said Mother Thomas. Her tone was calm and frank.

"You've been tramping the whole night long?" He watched us warily, and I felt it was only a matter of moments before he'd sniff out the truth. But Mother Thomas continued as if all was perfectly normal.

"I'm taking Elspeth's niece to New York," said Mother Thomas, indicating me with a gesture. "Will you carry us there?"

Pruitt Jones stepped close and looked me over. I was surprised that as dirty as he appeared, he only smelled of the fresh air and salt sea.

"She doesn't look a thing like Elspeth," he said, and snorted. "Just as well! Elspeth is nothing but trouble, coming and going. But what are you doing over here in Bayville? Why isn't Noah taking you? Why didn't you ask the Fletcher boys to take ye to New York on their regular run?"

"Why should I give good money to those lazybones?" said Mother Thomas. "And risk my neck in their old washtub?"

Pruitt Jones grunted in agreement, but kept eyeing us suspiciously.

"The truth is, Pruitt," said Mother Thomas, and paused.

What was she going to tell him?

"Elspeth and Noah have acted rather badly toward Hope. So I'm taking her to other relations in New York. But I don't want all of Oyster Bay to know," said Mother Thomas.

It was a perfect lie because there was so much truth in it.

Pruitt looked at me and nodded. "Aye," he said, "you've a troubled look about you, girl. 'Tis a wonder you were sent here in the first place, Elspeth being what she is, and Noah —" He looked at Mother Thomas and broke off in midsentence. "But I'll be telling no tales, Maude," he said. "Family business is best kept in the family."

"Pruitt, even Noah isn't to know where we've gone."

Pruitt Jones looked at me again, took Mother Thomas's hand, and all the gruff and bluster left him.

"Anything you say, Maude. Should Noah come round, I'll not tell him any more than the time of day."

"I knew I could depend on you," said Mother Thomas.

If I hadn't been there, I think she might have kissed him.

"Will ye leave now?" asked Pruitt Jones.

"If we can?"

"The tide's right, the breeze is fresh," said Pruitt Jones. "I'll put on a bushel of my apples to sell in New York, and we can cast off whenever you like."

"Sooner is better than later," said Mother Thomas.

"Right," said Pruitt Jones. He ducked into his house and emerged moments later, lugging a bushel of apples. He pulled a stained and torn tricorn hat off a peg by the door. Once outside, he shut and locked the door with great care.

"I don't want to leave no welcome mat for those thieving Rebel raiders from Connecticut," he said. "Pity the dog died."

I could tell him something about thieving raiders — the Oyster Bay kind, if only I dared. But if I were ever to see my family again, I'd have to keep silent no matter what Pruitt Jones, or any other Tory, had to say.

Pruitt Jones went first down a steep path. I could tell the bushel gave him some trouble, but I couldn't offer help as I was struggling with the incline and my own burdens. We came to a small inlet where the shallop was anchored. I expected the boat would be as tattered as her captain, and was completely taken aback. The *Marianne* was the trimmest little sailing craft I'd ever seen. Every bit of brass on her shone golden and mirror bright. The white paint of the hull looked as fresh as this morning. The *Marianne* was writ in curvy golden letters, outlined with black. All the ropes and sailcloth were tied or stowed neatly. There wasn't a speck of dirt upon her. I was too stunned to board. Mother Thomas watched me, a smile playing about her eyes. She seemed to enjoy my amazement. Pruitt Jones did, too.

"Ha, ha, ha!" He laughed like a barking dog. "Just because I'm a miserable old man, you thought I'd not treat my lady with respect."

"I, I . . ." As I stammered out an answer, I felt the color rising to my cheeks.

"Don't tease her, Pruitt," said Mother Thomas. "You know that the *Marianne* comes as a surprise."

"That she does," said Pruitt Jones, still chuckling. "A bright, beautiful surprise."

We clambered on board. Pruitt Jones stowed the apples and hoisted the mainsail. The *Marianne* gracefully tacked out of the harbor and headed west into a stiff breeze. No matter what lay ahead, I was glad to be free of Oyster Bay. Pruitt Jones looked over at me and winked. And I laughed. I laughed in spite of the danger ahead. I laughed to think of the Rebel baggage Pruitt Jones was carrying aboard the beautiful *Marianne*.

7

New York

"We're rounding Corlear's Hook, Girl," said Pruitt Jones in my ear. "Ye don't want to sleep through this view of New York Harbor!"

I sat up quickly, rubbing my eyes. I hadn't meant to sleep at all, but the labors and anxiety of the night and the past weeks caught up with me, and I'd fallen into a worried sleep soon after we set sail.

I rubbed my eyes again, trying to take in the scene before me. Father had come often to New York before the war, but I'd never seen it, and his descriptions couldn't have prepared me for *this* New York. Mighty British warships dominated the harbor, with cannons bristling from long rows of portholes. There were also fat merchant ships; flocked round them were small craft loading and unloading cargo.

"Mercy," said Mother Thomas. "New York's changed much more than I'd thought."

"Aye," said Pruitt Jones. "The war's been the unmaking and making of New York. The fire near destroyed her, but there's more trade, more money now than ever."

The closer we got, the more I could see that the wharves and docks were every bit as crowded and busy as the harbor. There were merchants, clerks, and workmen aplenty. Carters, drovers, and stevedores hauled heavy goods back and forth from boat to dock to warehouse. The commerce made a lively scene, but I couldn't be much interested, because for every plain-clothed person, there seemed to be two or three red-coated British soldiers!

"Do ye mark the big stone buildings there ahead?" asked Pruitt Jones.

"Aren't those the sugar refineries?" said Mother Thomas.

"They were," Pruitt Jones said, and spat over the side. "Now they're prisons for Rebel trash and other traitors to the Crown."

I shuddered and Mother Thomas took my hand. How could I set foot upon this terrible shore?

"Isn't it good to be on the way home, Hope?" said Mother Thomas.

She was right. I was on my way. Somehow I'd have to

see beyond the British soldiers to that end — my home, my family.

"Yes," I said.

"Whereabouts in New York are Hope's kin?" asked Pruitt Jones. "I'll tie up and see you to her door, then take you back to Oyster Bay, Maude."

"Thank ye, no," said Mother Thomas. "We can manage fine on our own. I'll be staying on a bit in New York."

"So that's how it is?" said Pruitt Jones.

"Aye," said Mother Thomas.

Pruitt Jones searched Mother Thomas's face, then nodded as though confirming something he'd seen there.

"I've often thought that there ought to have been a better home for Maude Thomas than what Noah's provided," he said. "A woman of quality tucked up in a garret with the potatoes, and that Elspeth working you like a . . ."

"Pruitt, please," said Mother Thomas.

"I'm glad you're moving on, but I don't like leaving you alone in a city filled with foreigners," said Pruitt Jones, eyeing a passing file of Hessian soldiers in their bright blue uniforms.

"Nonsense, Pruitt," said Mother Thomas. "They are here to protect us."

"Begging your pardon, Maude. But soldiers is soldiers. A fine-looking woman and a young girl ought to take care."

Mother Thomas smiled up at him, and the years left her face. "Thank ye for your concern, Pruitt," she said. "We will take care. Now, how much do I owe you?"

"Nothing today," he said. "It was an honor to have you aboard."

Mother Thomas started to protest.

"No, truly, Maude. I cannot charge ye. I am only proud you sought my help. Besides, I'll sell my apples, pick up some copies of the *Royal Gazette*, and sell them back in Oyster Bay."

"Thank you," said Mother Thomas. She stretched on tiptoe to plant a kiss on his weathered cheek.

Pruitt Jones coughed and sputtered, his face turning red. "Well, when you have need of me, come looking at this slip. Or leave a message at the Sailor's Arms."

Mother Thomas picked up her grip, and I the two satchels. "Do you see the Sailor's Arms, Hope?" he asked, pointing down the street to the painted sign of a schooner in full sail.

"Aye," I said.

"Don't forget," said Pruitt Jones, leaning down so we were eye to eye. "Call on me whenever there is need."

I very nearly asked him, then and there, to take us to Connecticut. But I stopped myself in time, remembering his opinion of Rebels.

"Thank you, sir," I said. "And thank you for taking us aboard the beautiful *Marianne*."

"Come along, Hope," said Mother Thomas.

We left Pruitt Jones standing on the pier next to the *Marianne*. When we'd gone a ways down the street, I turned to see him following us with his eyes. Mother Thomas didn't turn to look or wave. She marched forward, but I saw her pull a hanky from her sleeve and dab her eyes. Now was not the time, but someday I'd ask her about Pruitt Jones. Meanwhile, I wanted to know where we were going.

"Is it far?" I asked.

"What, dear?"

"Are we going far?"

"No, just a few streets. Mrs. Doyle lets rooms on the north end of Pearl Street. We shall board with her while we make arrangements to get to Bedford."

"Then we cannot leave today?" I was sorry the minute I said it, seeing the look of complete exhaustion on Mother Thomas's face.

"No, Hope," she said. "It may take a little time. We'll need a place to stay."

"I didn't mean . . ." I owed her so much, I didn't want Mother Thomas to think I was ungrateful. "Couldn't I carry the grip for you, now?"

"I can manage," she smiled. "Hope, would you mind being my orphaned granddaughter from now on? It will seem more natural for us to be together and no one will question it."

"I'd be pleased, Grandmother," I said, and we continued on.

As I followed Mother Thomas, I looked about me, trying to take in New York Town. Tall houses and shops were crowded up against each other without a hair's breadth in between. Many of the houses had odd-looking stepped gables facing the street. Once we got a few streets in from the wharves, there weren't as many soldiers and sailors about. In fact, there were plenty of fashionable ladies in gowns of silk, their hair piled high, curled and powdered. The gowns were quite beautiful, but I'm glad Mother didn't dress her hair so piled up on top of her head. Not only did it look ridiculous, it must have been a great deal of trouble, as well. There were other women in bright-colored, embroidered dresses of a type I'd never seen before, who spoke a strange language.

"Those are the wives of the Hessian soldiers," said Mother Thomas when I pointed them out. "There are plenty of foreigners in New York, always have been, especially Dutch. Of course, the Dutch were here first."

There were also many men, women, and children in rags who hawked sad-looking wares, or begged. Servants hurried along, carrying packages and firewood. Some ran down the street taking empty buckets to the water pump at the corner, while others labored back up the street, their buckets filled.

I was surprised at the number of shops. Each had a gaily painted sign showing its wares: gloves, cookware, fancy cakes, boots, chairs and chests, bonnets, and on and on. But all the bright and fancy things were set against a filthy backdrop. The streets were strewn with garbage. Pigs squealed and shoved each other as they foraged in the debris. Drivers in carriages and riders on horseback were obliged to go around them, or wait while the pigs fed.

I'd never been anyplace so busy, crowded, and dirty before. If all went well, we'd be leaving soon, before Mr. Thomas could track us down. Left to his own devices, I thought he'd be too ashamed to go after his own mother. But I could count on Elspeth's greed and lack of feeling to push him into pursuit. I sighed.

"Not much further," said Mother Thomas.

How my arms ached, and my feet and legs. Each and every part of me was longing for rest. All at once I felt that to walk one more step was beyond endurance.

"Hope," said Mother Thomas. "Hope, this is Mrs. Doyle's house."

Mother Thomas beckoned to me from the doorstep of a cream-colored clapboard house, trimmed in green and black peeling paint. The shiny brass knocker summoned a serving girl in a starched apron and cap.

"We're looking for lodgings," said Mother Thomas.

"Then you're in great luck," said the girl. "New York is so crowded it's about to burst, but two guests left here this morning."

She showed us into the chilly parlor and went to fetch Mrs. Doyle. We sat on either side of the empty grate, on two high-back rush chairs. I set down my burdens and sat still, numb with tiredness.

The parlor was an ample room, sparsely furnished with a few side chairs, small tables, and one fine desk in the corner. Everything was orderly, but not quite clean. On the wall opposite me was a matched set of paintings. One was of a young, plump mother holding a tightly swaddled staring babe. The other showed a gentleman dressed in merchant's black, sitting at an open window where a ship could be seen in the harbor.

"How do ye do?" said Mrs. Doyle, bustling into the room. "I see you've made the acquaintance of Mr. Doyle and my precious son, both lost to me." She looked at the paintings and sorrowfully shook her head. "Dear, dear."

I stood up quickly and my legs nearly gave way.

"Sit, child," said Mrs. Doyle. "You look ready to fall."

It wasn't proper to sit while a grownup stood, but Mother Thomas nodded and I sank back on the chair.

"We've had a long weary journey to your doorstep," said Mother Thomas.

"Poor things! I'll have Polly fetch you a cup of tea." Mrs. Doyle was out the door and back again in a moment. She pulled up a tea table and a chair, and all the time she was hurrying about, she kept up a freshet of chatter.

"Well, I should think! Poor child can't even stand. You both look positively done in. Where are you coming from? No doubt the Rebels forced you out, as they have so many Loyalists. And where do they all come? New York, of course! Dear, dear, what terrible times!"

Polly came in with a tea tray laden with brown bread and a tiny pot of apple butter. We hadn't had tea at home since the Tea Party in Boston Harbor. Mother often lamented its absence, but Patriots had sworn not to drink tea until King George's taxes were repealed. Now I was in Loyalist New York, pretending to be loyal to the king, and I was so hungry and thirsty, I felt able to drink a harborful of the king's tea without regret.

Mother Thomas took a sip and sighed with satisfaction. Mrs. Doyle cut thin slices of bread, put a dab of apple butter on each plate, and chattered on like a plump, busy squirrel.

"Have some apple butter and bread, baked this morning. We usually bake on Saturday. But there was no flour to be had Saturday. And if it weren't for our own little apple tree, we'd have naught to serve a sweet tooth. What did you say your name was?"

"I beg your pardon, I am Mrs. Jacob Jones. This is my granddaughter, Hope."

Mother Thomas lied without batting an eye. I was taken aback, though it made sense not to use "Thomas" should Noah come looking. But I wondered why she'd chosen "Jones."

"Hope! What a comfort to you. If only my hopes were still alive." She pointed to the paintings. "That is all I have left of Mr. Doyle and my only child." Tears filled her eyes and coursed down her plump cheeks.

"I'm so very sorry," said Mother Thomas.

"They were both killed by the Rebels in the Battle of New York. My boy was only sixteen. They are dead and gone, and I remain, seeing it all go to rack and ruin." She blew her nose and wiped her eyes.

Father had fought against the British in the Battle of New York. Many Patriots had died in the process, and many more were captured. I'd never before had a thought for the British nor the Loyalists who'd fought and died. Here I was drinking this kind woman's tea, and, for all I knew, Father or one in his command had killed her husband or son. I swallowed hard as the bright-eyed babe stared out at me from the painting.

"But tell me about yourselves," said Mrs. Doyle.

"We come to you on the best recommendations of my friend, Mrs. Ellsworth, who stayed with you after the fire in the west ward consumed her home."

"Ah, Mrs. Ellsworth, poor dear," said Mrs. Doyle. "And does she well on Long Island?"

"Yes, very," said Mother Thomas.

"Why have you left the bounty of Long Island for the scarcity and uncertainty of New York?"

"Our stay with you will be brief," said Mother Thomas. "Only for as long as it takes to arrange for a carriage to take us to Bedford. Hope and I are going to family there."

"But, my dears!" said Mrs. Doyle. "I shall have you here a very long time. It is terribly dangerous in Westchester County. Much of it is a kind of no man's land. James De Lancey and his cowboys raid thereabouts, and many the innocent falls victim to them. The Rebel troops are even more vicious. Even if you survive the cowboys and Rebels, the roads are in such a state, I doubt anyone would risk his animals, his axles, nor his own skin on them."

I looked to Mother Thomas, who had two sharp lines of worry etched on her brow. And yet her voice was steady.

"I'm sure we will find a way," she said. "It is most important that we get to Bedford."

"Just the same," said Mrs. Doyle. "I think you'd best take the weekly rate."

A week would give Elspeth all the time in the world to find us, all the time in the world.

8

Marooned

"Any luck this morning?" asked Polly, looking up from her pie making as I entered the kitchen.

"None," I said. Every day for over a fortnight Mother Thomas and I had tried, unsuccessfully, to hire a carriage to take us to Bedford. Mother Thomas still believed our plan would succeed; we *would* find a way to Bedford, her cousins would then take me on to Grandmother Burr's. I began to worry if Mother Thomas's cousins were still *there*. The war had brought so many changes. Would a Loyalist family stay on in Bedford? Mother Thomas assured me that her family had always been well liked in Bedford, and would not leave, nor be made to leave.

I had other fears, as well, trudging from one end of the town to the other, unable to find a carriage, that we'd be marooned in New York. And each day that we were delayed, there was the stronger chance that Mr. Thomas would appear and take us both back to Oyster Bay.

"Don't worry, Hope. Pruitt Jones won't tell a soul where we've gone," said Mother Thomas. "There never was a truer friend. Noah won't have figured out where we've gone on his own, and if he does, I hope he'd be too ashamed to come after us."

Elspeth could figure it out, and she wasn't ashamed to do anything. It might take time, but she could make him come after us.

"Where did you go today?" asked Polly.

"We heard of a farmer with a horse and wagon on the Broadway, halfway to Greenwich Village."

"And was there a wagon?"

"There was an *old* horse and a rickety wagon." I tied on an apron and took up a bowl of apples and a paring knife. Mother Thomas and I helped Mrs. Doyle with cooking and housework for a reduction in our board. "Do you want these sliced or minced?"

"Sliced fine," said Polly. "So what did the farmer say?"

"What every other man with a horse and carriage has said to us: 'The roads never were that good. Now they're impassable.' 'Even the post riders have trouble getting through.' 'Those Rebel brigands will confiscate

77

a Loyalist's horse and carriage.' 'Why go to the north, anyway? It's plagued by Rebel raiders.' "

Polly shook her head. "It's too bad for you, Hope. I know your heart is set on getting to your cousins in Bedford."

I still had nightmares about my family being out in the cold, hungry and sick. But during the day, I forced myself to believe that they were safe in Litchfield with Grandmother Burr. I had thought to be with them in time to celebrate Thanksgiving. Father might have gotten leave for the holiday, especially if General Washington knew of what had befallen our family. I had imagined the day so clearly, Grandmother's huge kitchen filled with the smells of roasting turkeys, cornbread and pies warming in the oven, and spiced apples stewing on the hearth. All the terrible days and nights since the raid might be forgotten in the happiness of being together. I needed so much to hear my sisters laugh again, to blot out the memory of their cries and mine that dreadful night.

But the day of Thanksgiving in Connecticut had come and gone, and I couldn't tell Polly, nor Mother Thomas, how it grieved me. At least there was no Thanksgiving celebrated in New York this year. I couldn't have stood the pretense of giving thanks when I had so little to be thankful for.

When it became clear that it might be some time before I could be back in Connecticut, I decided to sell my pewter mug and use the money to send a letter to my family. Mother Thomas reluctantly approved my plan. A letter might have as difficult a time getting to Connecticut as ourselves. Mother Thomas didn't want me to waste any of my wealth on a futile effort. There was also the danger that my letter could get into the wrong hands and put us in jeopardy. But I had to try to let Mother know that I was safe and doing my best to get back to her.

We gave the New York postmaster a carefully worded letter to my mother in care of Grandmother Burr. He wouldn't promise when, or if, it could be delivered. A ship was headed upriver in a few days. The mail would be left at Tarrytown, and from there, I hoped, someone would take it on to Litchfield. The chances weren't very good, but doing something was better than doing nothing. I'd been thinking about my letter all day, every day since then, and hoping for a reply.

I gave Polly the sliced apples. She smiled and handed me another bowlful to peel and slice.

"I asked Grandmother Jones if we might buy a horse and ride it to Connecticut." I always thought twice before speaking, lest I say "Mother Thomas."

"Mrs. Jones does not look strong enough for that," said Polly.

"You're right, especially the past few days she seems quite low." I hadn't thought until that moment that

Mother Thomas had been looking very worn of late. Now she was lying in our bed instead of helping us in the kitchen. Usually our morning's tramp didn't fatigue her so.

"No matter," I said. "There's no one who could or would spare a horse, at least for what we could afford."

I regretted not asking Pruitt Jones for his help when I'd had the chance. Could he not sail to Fairfield one night, as Noah Thomas had done, and leave us ashore? But what if he were caught? Pruitt would be put in irons, and he'd lose the *Marianne.* That would, indeed, be too much to ask. I sighed and put down my knife.

"We thought it would be such an easy thing to go from New York to Bedford," I said. "Now I wonder if we shall ever leave this town."

Polly looked at me full of sympathy, and then her freckled face stretched into a wide grin.

"For my part, I'm glad to have you here," she said.

I managed a smile, too. Working alongside Polly was almost like going to a frolic every day. Mrs. Doyle didn't mind how much we chatted as long as the work got done. And she never set us a heavy task without also rewarding us with a trip down the street to the shops, or time to sit by the fire with our knitting. Polly was full of stories and laughter. I was sorry not to be more honest with her about my circumstances. But as much as I liked Polly, it was safer to keep my secrets to myself. When she told me tales about her brothers and sisters in New Jersey, I told her about Mary, Abigail, and baby Jonathan. I said they were my cousins in Rye. Polly asked me once how my parents died. I became so sad thinking of them, I could hardly speak. "They just died," I said, tears spilling out of my eyes. What if they *had* died, and I didn't know it? Polly didn't ask me about them again.

"Girls! Girls!" cried Mrs. Doyle, poking her head in at the back door. "Come and see what I've got."

We left off our tasks and hurried out the back door. Mrs. Doyle was standing by the chicken coop, gazing proudly at a strutting turkey.

"Isn't he a fine fellow? Won't he be the crown of our Christmas feast? Imagine finding such a beauty in New York, in these evil days!"

"However did you manage it?" asked Polly.

"It was quite a stroke, my dear," said Mrs. Doyle. "I shall have a cup of tea and tell you all about it. Isn't he grand, Hope?"

"It's a very fine bird," I said, hoping to sound excited and knowing that I didn't. We'd never celebrated Christmas; Congregationalists considered it a pagan holiday. But for the Anglicans of Fairfield, and for the Anglican Loyalists here, it was even more important than our Thanksgiving.

"Well, back to work, girls," said Mrs. Doyle. "We've still much to do to ready the feast for our little family."

Mrs. Doyle had eight other boarders besides ourselves. All were Loyalists who'd left their homes to come under King George's protection in New York. Dr. Jordan said his home in New Jersey had been burned down by angry Rebels. I couldn't imagine why anyone would do that to the kindly old gentleman and his frail wife. For that matter, why should anyone want to harm my own sweet mother? War was the answer. War allowed for all the unimaginable things. I believed with all my heart that the Patriots' cause was just; we had a right to be free. But I hated the war.

"Mrs. Kiggins and I were just going up the street to get a bit of ribbon for the new bonnet she's making." Mrs. Doyle was telling the tale of the turkey as she took sips of her tea and fluted a pie crust. "Poor, dear Mrs. Kiggins gets completely lost on her own. Hope, you've learned the streets so well; you must show her around."

I nodded. I had learned more about New York than I cared to know. Our daily jaunts had taken us all over, and I'd seen everything that was good and bad about the town. Some people were having a gay, elegant time in New York, to judge by their fine carriages and fashionable clothing, but most New Yorkers looked as if they were just scraping by.

Mrs. Kiggins was one of the people just getting by. She was a small, frightened woman who'd come here when her husband had joined the British forces. Having no family to shelter her, and not the means to keep their home in upstate New York, she'd come to New York to be with Loyalists, wait out the war, and try to earn an extra penny as a seamstress to the wealthy.

"Well, just as we were turning onto Platt Street, a wagon came toward us and the farmer asked could we direct him to General Tryon's house." Mrs. Doyle paused a moment and frowned at her pie crust. "Do you think three chicken pies will be enough, Polly?"

"Three chicken, two mince, two apple, one Marlborough pudding, one huckleberry, two pumpkin, and one currant," said Polly, counting on her fingers. "Enough pies I should think. But what about the farmer?"

"We got to talking," said Mrs. Doyle. "And it turned out that he had come all the way from Dutchess County and was distant kin to Mr. Kiggins!"

"Isn't that a marvel," said Polly.

"And when he heard about Mr. Kiggins serving under General Howe, and Mrs. Kiggins being here on her own, he let us have one of General Tryon's turkeys!"

"Fancy that!" said Polly.

"Naturally, I had to do a bit of fast talking," said Mrs. Doyle. "But, after all, the Tryons can spare *one* bird. No doubt they'll never miss it."

"No doubt," said Polly, winking at me. "It will be a real Christmas, war or no. Won't it, Hope?"

I forced myself to smile and nod. They were so pleased and only wanted me to be happy, too. But I couldn't be happy until I knew my family was well, and I was safely with them again.

"It's only December sixteenth," said Polly. "Hope may get to Bedford in time to keep Christmas with her cousins."

"We don't celebrate Christmas," I said without thinking, and instantly regretted my careless words.

"Not keep Christmas?" said Mrs. Doyle, looking at me quizzically. "But you are of the Anglican Church?"

I might as well have said outright that I was a Rebel captain's daughter.

"What I meant to say . . ." Think, Hope, *think.* "We . . . since my mother . . . She died on a Christmas Eve. Since then we've been too sad to celebrate Christ's birth."

"Poor dear," said Mrs. Doyle. "Sorry to bring up such a painful recollection. Leave off the mincemeat, and let me show you how to weave a fancy lattice for this huckleberry pie."

By the time the pies were out of the oven and lined up on the shelves in the freezing larder where they'd keep until Christmas, we were busy getting supper on the table. Moving from task to task in the warm steamy kitchen amongst these kind strangers eased my heart. Every day brought fresh disappointments and worries; at least I'd found a safe harbor until I could return to my family.

One by one, the boarders assembled in the kitchen for the evening meal. Mrs. Doyle said that during the warm months, dinner and supper were served in the parlor. Once the cold weather set in, formality was abandoned for comfort. There were fireplaces in nearly all the rooms of the house, but fuel was so scarce, the only fires kept burning were in the big kitchen hearth and the room of Dr. Jordan and his wife. And he provided his own firewood.

"Where ever is Mrs. Jones?" asked Mrs. Doyle. "I'm ready to serve the stew."

"Perhaps she's fallen in a doze," said Polly. "She looked so done in today."

"Run and fetch her, Hope," said Mrs. Doyle. "She needs her supper to keep up her strength."

I was already halfway up the staircase. I'd been happy to think of Mother Thomas getting some rest. Now I felt some alarm.

With all the boarders down in the glowing kitchen, the rest of the house was dark and quiet as a tomb. I felt my way up the stairs and along the landings to our room on the third floor. I hated these stairs, which tilted to one side and gave me the feeling that, without extreme vigilance, I would slide through the flimsy banisters and plummet to the floor below. I clung to the wall going up, and was grateful for the darkness that obscured the drop. By the time I reached our door, my eyes were somewhat accustomed to the gloom. Mother Thomas was in bed, her cloak spread on top of the covers and her shawl wrapped around her shoulders. I went to the bed and softly called her name.

"I am awake, Hope," she said in a voice as dry as sand.

"Supper is on the table, awaiting you."

"Send my regrets," she said. "I'll keep to my bed."

"Are you unwell?"

She looked at me with glistening eyes and nodded.

I touched her thin, knotted hands and brow. She was so hot, she might have been afire!

"I'll get Dr. Jordan," I said, and turned to run downstairs.

"Hope." Her hoarse voice stopped me. I sank beside her.

"Be brave," she whispered.

I ran down to the kitchen, not brave, only terribly frightened. I went directly to Dr. Jordan's chair.

"Good heavens, Hope!" said Mrs. Doyle. "What is the matter? You're as pale as death."

"Please, come." I took hold of Dr. Jordan's hand.

He got right up from the table. Polly was quick to

light a candle to brighten our way, and yet it seemed to take an impossibly long time to get back to Mother Thomas.

Polly walked in first and set the candle on the bedside table. Mother Thomas turned toward the light, to face us. Polly stepped back, crying out, "Lord in heaven, preserve us. It's the pox!"

9

The Pox

"She can't stay," cried Mrs. Doyle. "She'll infect the whole house. Oh, dear! What a dreadful thing!"

Mrs. Doyle stood on the landing outside our room. Polly stood behind her, weeping into her apron. Dr. Jordan sat by the bed, gently holding Mother Thomas's thin wrist between his thumb and ring finger. Meanwhile, he gazed thoughtfully at the watch he held in his other hand. I stood beside Dr. Jordan, not in his way, but where I could see Mother Thomas. And her fever-bright eyes never left mine.

"Imagine, the *pox* in my house!" Mrs. Doyle sobbed.

"And your only family is in Bedford?" Dr. Jordan asked me quietly.

I started to say something, but Mother Thomas kept looking at me steadily and shook her head. "None but them," she said, her voice rasping.

Wouldn't she want to be with her son? As much as I feared the arrival of Mr. Thomas, wouldn't the only *right* thing be to send him word of his mother's illness? But Elspeth. Elspeth wouldn't have Mother Thomas, sick with smallpox, in her house.

"You're very ill, madam," said Dr. Jordan, his voice pitched low so that only Mother Thomas and I could hear him. "Mrs. Doyle has reason to fear for herself and her lodgers."

The pox hadn't come to Fairfield that I could remember. But Mother, Father, and Grandmother Burr told sad stories of its effects. Grandmother's sister, her husband, and all their children were stricken and only Cousin Anne survived. I knew enough to be as terrified as Mrs. Doyle, but not enough to know what lay ahead. I did know we needed help.

"We've nowhere to go," I blurted out.

"I know of a kind woman, a *good* nurse," said Dr. Jordan. "She runs a house in Greenwich Village, especially for those taking the smallpox inoculation. She is immune to the pox, as are all her servants. She can offer you a clean, safe place, and skilled nursing."

I had heard of pox houses. Mother and Father had debated whether or not it was worth the risk to take the inoculation.

"What about Hope?" asked Mother Thomas.

Dr. Jordan turned and drew me closer to the flickering candlelight. He studied my face and felt my forehead with the back of his cool, dry hand.

"She seems well enough, now," he said. "But as you've been sharing a bed, it's most likely Hope will also contract the smallpox."

He spoke so calmly. Mother Thomas, as sick as she was, also seemed calm. But I was not. I wanted to shriek and sob like Mrs. Doyle, or at least to weep like Polly. But I didn't shriek, sob, nor weep. I hugged myself to stop shaking, and listened as my fate was being settled.

"Will it be better for her to stay with me?" asked Mother Thomas.

Dr. Jordan shrugged. "I don't know that Mrs. Doyle will let her stay."

"Will your friend take us both in?"

"I'm sure Mrs. Willows will accommodate you both," said Dr. Jordan.

"Will it be very dear?"

"As Mrs. Willows is out in the country, her expenses are not so great. I don't believe it will cost more than what Mrs. Doyle charges you."

But who knew for how long we'd have to stay with her? Mother Thomas had insisted on paying for our board with Mrs. Doyle. I was already worried that her money would run out before we could get to Bedford. I had my family's silver and pewter. That would pay for our keep and nursing, but not forever.

Mother Thomas's eyes sought mine. "Very well," she said. Her eyes closed and her thin face sank back against the pillows. "Please make the arrangements for us."

I followed the doctor onto the landing.

"She's so sick," I said. "Won't it do her harm to be moved?"

Dr. Jordan looked at me over his glasses, his eyes clouded. "I don't think it will matter," he said.

Of course it would matter. Even I knew that a sick person shouldn't be taken out in the cold.

Dr. Jordan took my hand. "Your grandmother is very ill. You must be prepared for the worst."

I shook my head. Mother Thomas was *not* going to die. It couldn't be a possibility. She'd left her family and taken on enough hardship to help me. She simply could not suffer anything else. God wouldn't allow it.

"Well, Doctor?" asked Mrs. Doyle. "What's to be done?"

"I shall have Mrs. Jones and Hope moved to Mrs. Willows's pox house in Greenwich Village."

Mrs. Doyle clasped her hands in prayer. "Thank you, Doctor, thank you!" she said. "Tonight?"

"Yes, tonight, if Polly will take a message to the Dover Street stables."

"At once, at once!" said Mrs. Doyle. She turned to Polly. "Run and get your cloak, then report to the doctor. And don't keep the good man waiting." She hustled Polly down the stairs.

I touched the doctor's sleeve. "Is there nothing I can do to make her more comfortable?"

"Indeed," said Dr. Jordan. "I'll give Mrs. Doyle some willow bark to brew. She knows how to make the decoction. Cool the fever with a damp compress, and warm Mrs. Jones when she's chilled. Take some firewood from my room. And, Hope . . ."

"Yes, Doctor?"

"Trust in the Lord and Mrs. Willows. He will point the way, and she will know what to do."

"Yes, sir."

He patted my shoulder and went down the stairs to his rooms to write the note for Mrs. Willows. I went back to Mother Thomas, who lay still with eyes closed.

"I'll just fix you some tea and come right back," I said. "Only water, Hope," she said. "And take the candle. It hurts my eyes."

I quickly extinguished the flame and crept down the stairs to the kitchen.

Everyone gathered around the table fell silent when I entered the room. Polly hurried past me in her cloak and bonnet. Her look was filled with pity and fear. I avoided her eyes and those of the others as well.

"Poor Mrs. Jones!" said Mrs. Doyle. "But Mrs. Jordan says that Mrs. Willows is the best nurse Dr. Jordan has ever known."

I couldn't answer. Mrs. Doyle meant well enough. But no amount of nursing could make up for the dangers of moving someone as sick as Mother Thomas.

"Mrs. Doyle, will you, please, brew the willow bark Dr. Jordan gives you for my grandmother? He says it will bring her ease."

"Certainly, Hope," she said. "I'll send Polly up with it as soon as she's back from the stables." Then her voice dropped to a whisper. "But she mustn't bring it into Mrs. Jones's room."

"Of course," I said. "Polly can leave it by the door."

"And, Hope, it's best you stay out of the kitchen."

"Yes, ma'am," I said, and ran back up the stairs with a jug of cold water from the pump.

When I returned to Mother Thomas she was in a fitful doze. She woke enough to swallow a sip of water, and then fell back against the pillows. I sat by her side, watching over her restless sleep. I cooled her brow and wrists with a damp cloth as I'd seen Mother do when she tended the fevers of Mary or Abigail. I should have been packing our few possessions, getting ready to go. But I could not bestir myself. I sat in the cold, dark room, too fearful to move, overwhelmed by this new danger for Mother Thomas and myself. Would it be better to die now, rather than live through the misery ahead? I sat quite still, wrapped in black despair, listening to the labored rise and fall of my friend's breath. Slowly, I became aware of another sound in the room — the steady *tick-tick* of Mother's precious clock. *Tick-tick.* It hadn't faltered once since we were taken from Fairfield. If only I could be so steady.

I had thought that the most difficult part of my journey home was behind me, the escape from Oyster Bay. Now, I could look back on that fearful night as difficult, yet exhilarating. Our plan had worked. But we'd made it safely away from Oyster Bay only to be becalmed here in New York.

If only the *Marianne* were waiting at the end of this night to take us safely to Connecticut. Wouldn't Pruitt Jones help Mother Thomas if he knew how much she needed him?

Mother Thomas groaned and I leaned forward to cool her brow. Her eyes fluttered open, and even in the dark, I could see her struggle to smile.

Pruitt Jones and the *Marianne* could not help us. There could be no glorious escape from smallpox. We were in the Lord's hands.

Mrs. Willows's black servant, Moses, carried Mother Thomas down the stairs in his arms as if she were a small child. He settled her gently in the back of the wagon, made soft with a thick layer of straw and supplied with two warm quilts. We'd need the warmth; the December night was black and stinging cold. I climbed in next to Mother Thomas, placing the canvas bags and her leather grip along the back of the wagon.

Dr. Jordan came out of the house to make sure Mother Thomas was as comfortable as possible.

"I will come to see you in a few days," he said. "Sooner, if Mrs. Willows sends for me."

I nodded. Mother Thomas was too ill to have heard or understood.

Dr. Jordan spoke a few words to Moses. Polly waved to me from the doorway. The wagon lurched forward, taking us down a winter road that might leave me forever out of reach of my family. I didn't kick or scream as I had when Mr. Thomas took me from my mother. I wanted to, but I didn't.

I cradled Mother Thomas's head in my lap, trying to save her from the jostling of the wagon. Since we'd discovered her illness only a few hours before, she'd grown steadily worse. There were many spots on her face and her fever had become delirium. Mother Thomas was so ill she no longer knew if it was day or night. Polly had been afraid to come as far as the landing to our room. Mrs. Doyle and the other lodgers kept at an even greater distance. Only Dr. Jordan came near us. But he'd already had the pox, and was immune. I was as frightened as Polly. But it didn't matter. I couldn't and wouldn't be parted from my friend. I held her dear head and prayed for her and myself.

Both Mother Thomas and Father had said, "Be brave." I didn't feel at all courageous — less so now than ever. But I would try. I would believe that although going to Mrs. Willows's would mean a delay in getting back to my family, Mother Thomas and I *would* continue on. The sickness would pass. I'd nurse her through it as I'd helped nurse Mother after Jonathan was born. I wouldn't let myself think what would happen if I sickened. I wouldn't think of the plagues of smallpox that had carried off all of Mother's cousins but one. Smallpox killed, but I would not think of that. I would try to be as steady as Mother's clock. And I would try not to think at all.

The wagon moved slowly to the edge of town, then slowed more as we followed the rutted Greenwich road past meadows and swamp. Every once in a while I could make out the darker shadow of a house or barn. There may have been many more; I couldn't tell. For all was shrouded in thick night that held the threat of snow. Eventually, I sank beside Mother Thomas, holding her in my arms, and fell asleep.

10
Mrs. Willows's

I woke up in a trundle bed and felt warm for the first time since I'd been taken from my home. A fire was burning in the grate. A tall woman, thick as a bear, her back to me, was tending a pot set on a trivet over glowing coals, to one side of the hearth.

Whatever she was brewing smelled wonderful, like early spring. I was content to lie still, breathing in its magic. I could tell Mother Thomas was in the bed above me by the sound of her harsh breathing, and I could see her thin, bent hand on the edge of the bed. The room was small, clean, the daylight kept at bay by gingham curtains. Everything seemed dainty in the room because the woman at the hearth took up so much space. I heard muffled voices and footsteps from other rooms, and wondered how many other people were in the house.

"Awake, are you?" she asked in a deep rumbling voice, without turning around.

"Yes," I said.

"Tea?"

"Yes, please."

I'd never been served in bed at home, except when I was very sick.

It would be more proper for me to get up, but I felt shy. So I stayed abed while the giant woman with eyes in the back of her head poured me a mug of tea.

Her face was less frightening than her broad back. It was stern, but also kind. I sat up and she handed me the mug.

"You are Hope," she said. "And I am Mrs. Willows."

I nodded. "Dr. Jordan told me to trust you," I said.

"He's right."

"How is my grandmother this morning?"

"Not well," she said. "But it is too soon to know how she'll fare." She folded her arms across her massive chest and regarded me intently.

I was still and waited for what might follow.

"We don't know what to do with you," said Mrs. Willows. Her mouth was set in a hard line, but her voice wasn't harsh. She turned back to tending her pot, and I waited for her to speak. I sipped the sweet tea. The fire crackled, the brew bubbled, the waiting was equally anxious and comfortable.

Mrs. Willows cleared her throat and spoke. "Dr. Jordan thinks you should take the inoculation. Otherwise, you will surely get the pox naturally, and that is much worse. Lord, don't I know."

One way or another, I was going to get the pox. I'd known it the moment I'd first seen the spots on Mother Thomas's face. I was grateful Mrs. Willows's back was turned. I didn't want to face anyone, let alone a total stranger, while I tried to accept my fate.

"Do you have an opinion?" asked Mrs. Willows, still with her large impassive back to me.

I'd never before been asked to give my opinion on so serious a matter. When Mother and Father had discussed inoculation before Jonathan was born, it seemed to be dangerous, but not nearly as deadly as contracting smallpox naturally. Mother and Father hadn't gone through with the inoculations because they felt that Mary and Abigail were too young, and Mother too sickly to risk it. I was not too young, and in spite of the hardships of the past weeks, I was strong and healthy. I would do what was right, what was sensible, what I thought Father would choose for me, even if it was the last thing I wanted to do.

"I . . ." I took a deep breath and began again. "I will take the inoculation."

Mrs. Willows nodded. At length she turned back to face me.

"Will it hurt?" I asked.

"It is only a scratch," she said. "I am a good nurse. And you'll get through the sickness all right." She looked at me kindly, and I felt, more than ever, like crying.

"Dr. Parks is coming this morning to inoculate the lady who came here yesterday. I shall ask him to tend to you as well."

"How much will the inoculation cost?"

"As the doctor will have already made the journey here to attend the lady, he shouldn't charge you more than a shilling."

I had two shillings left over from the sale of my pewter mug.

"And when will I sicken?"

"In a week, perhaps two," said Mrs. Willows. "If you help me nurse your grandmother, the time will pass more quickly."

"I'd like to help," I said, and hastened to get up.

Mrs. Willows was busy at the hearth while I dressed. I made myself as neat as possible and stood by Mother Thomas. She was still in a fitful sleep. She tossed upon her bed and uttered low, hoarse moans. I touched her hot hand and her eyes opened briefly. But I don't think she saw me.

"How old is your grandmother?" asked Mrs. Willows.

I had no idea how old Mother Thomas was. I said, "Fifty-nine." That was the age of Grandmother Burr, and less a lie than most I'd told since coming to loyalist New York.

"She seems a deal older than that," said Mrs. Willows, coming over to the bed carrying a cup of her heady brew. "But a hard life will age a person." She looked down at me and sighed. "She is your only family?"

"We were trying to get to our cousins in Bedford," I said.

"Bedford? To get through Westchester County is near impossible these days, there is so much raiding and fighting. Perhaps we can send your cousins a letter," said Mrs. Willows. "But I don't know if the post riders will go that way at all anymore."

Had my letter found its way beyond Tarrytown, to Litchfield?

Mrs. Willows handed me the warm herb brew. Then she leaned over Mother Thomas and spoke softly in her ear. "We're going to sit you up and help you drink this. It should bring you some relief." She skillfully, and gently, drew Mother Thomas to a more upright position, and propped pillows behind her head and back to keep her supported. Then she spoke to me. "See if you can get Mrs. Jones to drink a few spoonfuls. It will do her some good."

"And make her well?"

"Nay," said Mrs. Willows. "Only God can make her well. I hope to bring her some ease."

I wanted Mrs. Willows to tell me Mother Thomas would get well, but I dared not ask because I couldn't bear to hear the truth.

"We will do what we can for your grandmother," said Mrs. Willows. "I'll call you when Dr. Parks arrives." And she left the room.

Mother Thomas was awake enough for me to spoon a few drops of Mrs. Willows's potion between her parched lips. I cooled her hot brow with scented water. She took a few more drops, then pushed the spoon away and shook her head. I moved the pillows that she might lie more easily, and continued to sponge her brow. I was glad to have a few moments alone. I needed time to try to understand it all. I'd never before seen anyone as sick as Mother Thomas. It frightened me that she was so sick, and that I was now the one in charge. I would have to make all the decisions and arrangements for us both. Being the oldest, I was used to taking care of Mary and Abigail, but this differed from bossing around two little sisters. I'd have to decide about our future. I'd have to try to find a way back to Connecticut on my own. But first, we'd both have to get beyond the pox.

If only I could go back to the first moment when everything went wrong and change it. I'd go back to that night in November. I'd keep the dogs from barking; I'd keep Mr. Thomas and his men away from our door. Perhaps I'd have to go back before that, and stop the war from happening in the first place. But how could I do that?

If Mr. Thomas could have known how little he'd profit by his deed, and how much his mother would suffer, he'd not have come raiding in Connecticut, would he?

All that was done and couldn't be undone, no matter how much I wished to change it. I'd have to carry on in spite of all that had happened — and all that was happening now. The doctor would come soon, and he would put the poison of smallpox into my skin. I would have to sit still and *let him do it!* How could I manage the courage to do that?

Mother Thomas seemed to be breathing better, and her sleep was deeper. Mrs. Willows's potion was working. Mother Thomas would get well. She had to.

There was a knock at the door. I stood and smoothed my skirts with fear-damp hands.

Be brave, be brave, be brave, I told myself. And I went to open the door.

11

Lady De Lancey

A cinnamon-colored woman was at the door.

"I'm Hitty," she said. "I've come to stay with your grandmother."

I had nearly become used to people calling Mother Thomas my grandmother, but Hitty, who looked very like Grandmother Burr's servant Rachel, reminded me that my true family was far away. I stared at her, wondering if there was some magic at work, and this really *was* Rachel.

"Missy?" Hitty was standing at the door, waiting for me to admit her.

"I'm sorry," I said. "Please come in."

She walked into the room, sat by Mother Thomas, and took her hand.

"Any change?" she asked.

"She seems to be resting better."

"That's all to the good," said Hitty. "The doctor's here. You'd better go on down to the parlor. The lady isn't very patient."

"The lady who's also being inoculated?"

"Yes, that lady," said Hitty.

I patted Mother Thomas's hand, took a deep breath, and left the warm, sweet-smelling room to meet my fate.

A little boy in scarlet livery was waiting at the foot of the stairs to show me into the parlor. He looked as if he were standing at the bottom of an abyss, and I had to fling myself down to him. Only I didn't do any flinging. I walked slowly down the stairs, my knuckles white from my grasp on the stair railing. When I reached the boy, he bowed and solemnly opened the door for me. No one had ever bowed to me before.

When I entered the room, Mrs. Willows was in hushed conversation at the window with a man in a dark satin suit, whose hair was powdered and curled. On the other side of the room, sitting before the fire, was a lady of fashion looking as ethereal as heaven. She wore pale blue silk, with cloudlike snowy lace edging her bodice and sleeves. Her hair was also powdered and piled high on her head in curls and cascading ringlets. She smiled, and beckoned for me to come closer.

"How do you do?" she said, extending her long white hand.

I took her fingertips and curtsied as Grandmother Burr had once taught me. I hoped I didn't look as awkward as I felt.

"How charming to meet a Colonial child with manners," she said. "And aren't you a pretty one."

She leaned back to study me, and I was glad, in that moment, for all the trouble Mother Thomas had taken to dress me nicely. For this lady seemed to measure every inch of me in her critical gaze. Her finger traced my cheek. "Let's hope there will be little scarring." She shuddered, then remade her face with a warm smile. "I've been told about you and your grandmother. May I offer my sympathies, Miss Jones?"

"Thank you, milady," I said, nodding and bobbing. I'd never before seen anyone so elegant, so refined. Hitty and Mrs. Willows had called her a lady. I wouldn't have been surprised if she'd come directly from the court of George the Third.

"Milady!" she said. "How very droll. Yes, my dear Miss Jones, I shall be *your* Lady De Lancey."

I attempted another curtsy, to cover my confusion and embarrassment.

"I understand we are to be inoculated for the pox together," she said. "Are you as frightened as I?"

Although she spoke lightly, I didn't doubt her fears.

"Yes, milady," I said. "I am much afraid."

"I daresay we have reason to fear. Shall we be each other's courage?"

"I beg your pardon," I said. "I don't understand." I didn't see that I had enough courage to be of use to anyone, especially this grand lady.

"When Dr. Parks inoculates us, let us hold hands and look into each other's eyes, and *not* think about the pox."

Lady De Lancey was a puzzle to me. She spoke to me as if I were her equal, which I clearly wasn't. Was she teasing, or sincere? Or both? Perhaps the specter of smallpox had made equals of a British peer and a Patriot's daughter. Not that I thought Lady De Lancey would be so generous if she knew I was Hope Wakeman. But I would trust her ladyship for now.

"Thank you," I said. "You are very kind."

Lady De Lancey laughed, and then she summoned the doctor. "We are quite ready if you are, Dr. Parks."

She didn't sound at all mean, but Dr. Parks was spoken to as if he were the least serving boy. The doctor stepped forward quickly, with a slight bow.

"At once, madam," he said.

During the inoculation, Lady De Lancey held my hands so firmly, she was a shade away from hurting me. Her eyes held my own just as determinedly. I felt ensnared by her blue eyes. She very nearly did keep me from noticing the doctor. Then there he was, briskly pulling up my sleeve. He scratched my arm; I was too afraid of what he was doing to know whether or not it hurt. All the while Lady De Lancey had her viselike grip on my hands, and her eyes locked on mine.

Once it was over for us both, she paid the doctor with a small purse of silver. I offered him the shilling from the pocket under my apron. Lady De Lancey laughed again and told me to put away my money, the doctor had been adequately compensated.

"Don't forget, Pepito is to be inoculated, as well," she said.

"Directly, madam," said Dr. Parks.

Pepito was probably the little boy in scarlet. I wondered who was going to hold his hand and ease his fears.

"And you are to look in on Mrs. Jones, if it suits Mrs. Willows."

I wanted to protest, because we couldn't afford Mrs. Willows and this fancy doctor, but I didn't feel able to contradict her ladyship.

"I shall return to attend you if so needed," he said, bowing deeply.

"Yes, yes," she said.

Still bowing, the doctor left the room.

"Mrs. Willows," said Lady De Lancey. "You may serve dinner now."

As soon as she said dinner, I realized how hungry I was. I hadn't eaten since yesterday's breakfast. Neither had Mother Thomas. I wondered if Hitty was able to get her to drink more.

Mrs. Willows looked at her ladyship, inclined her head, then lumbered out of the room.

"I've heard she's the best nurse there is in New York," said Lady De Lancey, even before Mrs. Willows had closed the door behind her.

I didn't think I was meant to reply, so I kept still. I was completely confused by Lady De Lancey. She was so out of place in Mrs. Willows's simple room, and so different from anyone I might have expected to find in a pox house.

"This is *not* how I'd intended to spend my visit with my dear sister," said Lady De Lancey. "If it hadn't been for that wretched seamstress, giving me a fitting even though she was already sick with the pox. Imagine! Perhaps it's just as well. At least I had enough warning to get myself inoculated. There's so much filth and illness here; it's unavoidable. And they say with the inoculation the disease is very mild." She stroked her own smooth cheek as she had mine. Her gaze grew distant, and she was silent.

There was a knock at the door, and Mrs. Willows came in, followed by Pepito and another woman, carrying steaming trays. The table near the window was moved to the fireside, dressed in white damask, and set with dainty china, all of which looked as if it had come with Lady De Lancey. There was a roasted capon, a beef pie, a dish of spiced apples and yams, two sweet puddings, fine white bread, all surrounding the center-piece of a pyramid of fruits and nuts.

"We shall dine quite simply," said Lady De Lancey. "I could only bring a few of my things here. And Isabella is probably having difficulties managing in a new kitchen. But we shall get on all right, yes?"

I nodded again, dumbstruck. This wasn't a simple meal; in wartime, in New York, it was a feast.

Mrs. Willows left the room, once the table was properly arranged, without saying a word. The other woman, who must have been Isabella, stayed until Lady De Lancey dismissed her. Pepito remained to serve us. He carved slivers of meat from the capon, and spooned dainty portions of each dish onto our plates. Then he filled Lady De Lancey's goblet with wine, and my cup with cider. Lady De Lancey never looked at Pepito. Occasionally she gave him some command in a foreign tongue, perhaps Spanish. She didn't sound harsh, only coldly formal. With me, her ladyship was very friendly and attentive. She made sure my cup and plate were never empty. The food was delicious, and I was so hungry, but I could hardly enjoy it. Everything was so fancy. I'd only dined on china at Grandmother Burr's house. I worried every time my spoon clinked against the plate that I would break it. And worse, we were each given a delicate silver fork. Lady De Lancey deftly speared bits of meat and neatly brought them to her mouth. I had to chase food around my plate, trying to hook onto it without making too much noise. Then I worried about dropping the forkfuls onto my dress. Furthermore, Lady De Lancey asked me a steady stream of questions.

"You must tell me all about yourself, Miss Jones," she said. "We will become friends and help each other pass the long, tedious days ahead. Can you read?"

"Yes, ma'am."

"Excellent! Are you skilled at paper cutting?"

I nodded.

"Can you play piquet?"

"I beg your pardon," I said. "What is piquet?"

"The card game," said Lady De Lancey.

"Oh, no! Card playing is —" I'd almost said "sinful" and only caught myself just in time. Card playing was a sin in my family's house. No doubt an Anglican aristocrat wouldn't think so.

"Card playing is?" said Lady De Lancey.

"Card playing is unknown to me," I stammered.

"Well, I shall fix that!" she said. "How else shall we beguile the time?"

I knew I looked worried, but I didn't think her lady-ship noticed.

"Now tell me about your family," she said.

"Both my parents are in heaven," I said. Silently I prayed that God would not punish me by making my terrible falsehood come true.

"I'd been told you were an orphan. I, too, was orphaned at a tender age," said Lady De Lancey. "And you never had brothers or sisters?"

"No," I said. But I thought of Mary, Abigail, and Jonathan, and tears began to choke me.

"Neither did I," she said. "What a coincidence!"

I thought her ladyship had mentioned a sister earlier, but I must have been mistaken.

"Now tell me about your home."

"Gone," I said, barely able to speak.

"Gone?"

"Fire," I said, starting to weep in earnest.

"Fire!" she said, amazed. "Bloomingdale, my in-laws' home, was burned down by Rebels last year. I was there and only managed to escape in my nightdress! Miss Jones, we are fated to be friends; our stars have already traced the same routes through heaven. But I shan't ask anything more about the past. I see it is too painful. For me, as well."

Lady De Lancey handed me her delicate cambric handkerchief. "Now dry your eyes and have some pudding."

I wiped my eyes, stifling oceans of unshed tears, but I could no longer eat. And now I began to worry about how long I'd been away from Mother Thomas. What if she woke up? Wouldn't she be confused, perhaps frightened in this strange place?

"Miss Jones," said Lady De Lancey. "You're not doing justice to Isabella's admirable pudding."

"Forgive me," I said. "I'm concerned about Moth — my grandmother." I was so unnerved it was hard to keep up my pretense.

"But of course!" said Lady De Lancey. "She is the only close family you have left. Is she very ill?"

"Yes, milady."

"And you would feel better to be near her?"

"Yes, please."

"Then we shall retire to your grandmother's room to see how she fares. Now that we've been inoculated, the pox will not keep us away!" Lady De Lancey chirped some orders to Pepito, who rushed about the room collecting various things: a book, a deck of cards, a bag of knitting.

Was she really planning on sitting with me at Mother Thomas's bedside? Lady De Lancey said something else to Pepito and he opened a traveling chest and pulled out a large, brilliantly patterned shawl.

Lady De Lancey rose from her seat.

"Shall we go up, Miss Jones?"

I nodded, and led the way out of the room. It seemed her ladyship was determined to pass the time in my company. I should have been pleased to find a friend here, but Lady De Lancey's attentions filled me with misgivings.

12

A Warning

Hitty said sometimes there were as many as ten people taking the inoculation for the pox. At this time Lady De Lancey, her retinue, Mother Thomas, and I were the only guests — patients. As Mother Thomas was so ill, and Lady De Lancey so demanding, it was just as well.

For three days Mother Thomas was delirious, only occasionally waking enough to recognize me and attempt a smile. Hitty, Mrs. Willows, and I were constantly at her side in rotating shifts. Lady De Lancey also spent part of every afternoon by Mother Thomas. She read to her from the Book of Psalms. Sometimes Mother Thomas heard her enough to smile.

Mrs. Willows's brews brought Mother Thomas some restful sleep, but in no way altered the course of the disease. I clung to every hopeful crumb Mrs. Willows or Hitty uttered, and did my best to ignore the hard evidence before my eyes.

"Your grandmother is a fighter," said Hitty. "That is all to the good."

She could fight, but could she win? Mother Thomas had left her safe, if uncomfortable, home to help me. I couldn't bear to think she'd suffer more than she already had for her kindness.

Hitty was laying a new fire in the grate, and I had made up the trundle bed and was just sliding it under Mother Thomas's bed when I heard a horse in the yard. Within a few minutes Dr. Jordan and Mrs. Willows entered the room. He brought a chicken pie from Mrs. Doyle, and several skeins of wool spun by Polly for me to knit into warm stockings. We'd been so hurried out of Mrs. Doyle's house, amidst such fear, I was surprised and pleased they'd remembered us at all.

The doctor looked me over. He measured my pulse with his practiced hand, felt my neck and forehead, and asked if I had any pains.

"No pain, sir, only I am so tired. And I've done nothing to make me tired." Except listen to Lady De Lancey day and night, but I didn't say that.

"Hmm," said the doctor. He looked at my arm where I had the inoculation. There were three raised red bumps. "Coming along," he said. "Everything is as it should be. Mrs. Willows will take good care of you and see that you're comfortable."

I'd been so taken up with worry for Mother Thomas, I hadn't thought too much about my own coming illness. I was scared, but Hitty and Mrs. Willows were constantly reminding me that cases of smallpox when introduced by inoculation were mild. I mostly chose to believe them.

"Have you had word from your relatives?" asked Dr. Jordan.

"No, sir."

"We sent a letter two days ago," said Mrs. Willows. "We can't look for a reply for at least a week."

"If ever," said Dr. Jordan, "the post being what it is nowadays." Then he turned his attention to Mother Thomas.

I knew there would be no reply. I'd let Mrs. Willows address the letter to Mr. Josiah Jones of Bedford, knowing that no such person existed. For how could I send word to Mother Thomas's cousins that Mrs. *Jones* was gravely ill, and with her granddaughter, Hope, stranded in Greenwich Village, New York? And yet I was desperate to send to someone for help — to pin my hopes on something.

I wondered if Mother had gotten the letter I sent her. Even though it would be impossible, I wished *she* could come for me. Before the war, it hadn't been such a great undertaking. When she was a girl, Mother and Grandmother Burr had taken their carriage several times to New York to see the latest fashions from Europe and make special purchases. Before the war, Father went to New York on business as often as he went to New Haven. Now the distance between New York and Fairfield seemed as vast as the ocean. I didn't see how I could find a way across.

Dr. Jordan was sitting by Mother Thomas, who was too feverish to be aware of his presence. He held her wrist and frowned.

"How long has the pulse been like this?" he asked.

"Since Sunday early morning," said Mrs. Willows.

The doctor shook his head. I knew she was gravely ill, but Dr. Jordan and Mrs. Willows seemed aware of some new complication I couldn't guess at. Dr. Jordan finished his careful examination, then he stepped aside to confer with Mrs. Willows. I tried to hear as much as possible of what they said.

"I administered the dose of jalap and calomel," said Mrs. Willows. "The purge was effective and not too hard on Mrs. Jones."

"Good," said Dr. Jordan. "Now I am concerned about the pulse. We might try digitalis."

"Foxglove?" asked Mrs. Willows.

And the doctor said, "Yes."

Hitty asked me to help her apply cooling herb compresses to Mother Thomas's ravaged face, and I heard no more.

As the doctor was about to take his leave, I offered him a coin from my pocket, but he wouldn't allow it.

"No, child," he said. "I fear you will need every penny."

That was my fear, as well.

"I've nearly forgotten my other commission," said Dr. Jordan as he began a search through the pockets of his waistcoat, coat, and trousers. "A peculiar old sea dog turned up at Mrs. Doyle's house last night. Said he had a message for Maude Jones. Called himself Captain Pruitt Jones. Do you know him, Miss Jones? Is he a relative?"

Pruitt Jones! He'd found us! How did he know we'd borrowed his name? I didn't know whether I should admit to knowing him or not. Truth seemed the safest course.

"The name is coincidental," I said. There were enough Joneses in the world for that to be true. "He's an old friend of my grandmother's."

"He seemed most distressed to learn of your grandmother's illness. He left this for her. Under the present circumstances, it is best I give it into your care."

Dr. Jordan retrieved a letter from his inner coat pocket and handed it to me. It was very like Pruitt Jones. The letter appeared to be an old page of the *Royal*

Gazette. The once wrinkled paper had been smoothed out, refolded, and sealed with wax.

I thanked the doctor, and with shaking hands, I put the letter in the pocket under my apron and kept my hands there to hide my nervousness. I felt certain that a letter from Pruitt Jones did not portend well. As anxious as I was to know its contents, I didn't think I could stand any more bad news.

Once the doctor and Mrs. Willows had left the room, I went over to the light of the window. With my back turned to Hitty, I took out the letter and held the fearsome thing in my hand. "Maude Jones" was written in bold black ink across the lines of newsprint. For a moment I thought of waiting for Mother Thomas to waken enough to read the letter herself. That would be polite, but cowardly *and* stupid on my part. I broke the seal and opened the letter.

Pruitt Jones had written a few short lines across the printed page.

> *Dearest Maude,*
> *I wish you'd taken my name years ago. The Fletcher boys saw you in New York and told Noah. What can I do to help you?*
>
> > *Yours,*
> > *P.J.*

Take us away from here, I thought. Take us this very minute to the Connecticut shore. I was ready to run down the stairs, out the door, and all the way to New York Harbor to leap aboard the *Marianne*.

Mother Thomas moaned, and I put the letter back in my pocket. I wouldn't be going anywhere soon. I would write to Pruitt Jones at the Sailor's Arms. I didn't know what I'd tell him, nor what I'd ask for. Meanwhile, I'd ask for the Lord's help in healing Mother Thomas and keeping Mr. Thomas from finding us. I went to Mother Thomas's bedside.

"Bad news?" asked Hitty.

"Not good," I said.

"I'm sorry."

As there was no telling Hitty about Noah Thomas or Pruitt Jones, it was better to change the subject. Besides, I had questions about Dr. Jordan's visit.

"What was the doctor's concern about my grandmother's pulse?" I asked.

"He's worried that her heart is overtaxed by her illness."

"Is it?"

Hitty was quiet a moment, her brow wrinkled as if she was deciding what to tell me. Finally she spoke.

"Yes."

"But she could still be all right?"

Hitty shrugged. "Hope for the best, expect the worst."

"Her ladyship said the exact same thing yesterday," I said.

"Her ladyship?" asked Hitty.

"Lady De Lancey," I said.

Hitty looked at me and grinned.

"What is funny?" I asked.

"*Lady* De Lancey?"

I was trying not to look as put out as I felt. "But her ladyship told me . . . ," I said and bit my lip. She told me many things, which often turned out to be false. After three days of her constant company, I shouldn't have been surprised by any of her falsehoods. Her tale of being an orphan without brothers or sisters was completely untrue. How else could she have been staying with her *sister*, and writing letters to her "dear Mama"? Most of her stories were made up. Lying seemed to suit her. I didn't mind so much once I understood that she lied to everyone, not just me. In fact, I felt some kinship with her, for she was as caught up in her lies as I was in mine. Even so, I preferred to know the truth.

"She's not Lady De Lancey?"

Hitty smiled and shook her head.

"But everyone calls her Lady De Lancey."

"*You* call her that," said Hitty.

"So, who is she?"

"She's the daughter of a wealthy London merchant, married to young Oliver De Lancey, and sister to General Tryon's wife. She's well connected, but not a peer-ess."

Mother Thomas moaned and Hitty rushed to her side. She helped Mother Thomas to sit up a bit and offered her some cooled tea. I came forward to help, if I could, and see if Mother Thomas might be awake enough to know me.

There was a knock at the door. Pepito stood on the landing. Further questions about *Mrs.* De Lancey would have to wait. Pepito never spoke to me. I don't think he understood very much English. Hitty said he was Portuguese, as was Isabella, who stayed with him in the attic. In addition to cooking the fancy dishes Mrs. De Lancey favored, Isabella took care of Mrs. De Lancey's clothes and dressed her hair. And when Pepito wasn't serving his mistress, Isabella mothered him.

Pepito bowed. I fetched my shawl and knitting. His arrival was my signal to wait upon Mrs. De Lancey in her chamber, which I did every morning at eleven. We dined at twelve, and returned to Mother Thomas's room at two. Mrs. De Lancey was as regular as the town clock.

She still looked the very image of a titled lady. Each day she appeared in a different silk or satin gown, trimmed with ribbons and lace. Her hair was now more simply dressed and the powder had been washed out.

Her light brown curls were, perhaps, less fashionable, but more handsome. Today her gown was spring green trimmed with pink and white.

"Miss Jones," she said, beckoning me to the chair opposite hers, in front of the fire. "It is so dreadfully cold again today. Isn't it lucky we are confined indoors? Otherwise we'd have to be out paying calls in this bitter weather."

As Mrs. De Lancey had gone from merchant's daughter to titled lady, I had also risen a good deal in society. Somehow she'd ignored my simple clothes and country manners. I was cast as a young lady Loyalist, a member of her well-to-do set of acquaintances in New York. I let Mrs. De Lancey's pretense continue without comment. Yet, how silly it was pretending all this nonsense when Mother Thomas was so terribly ill, and any moment Mr. Thomas might break down the door and drag me away.

The fire was blazing, but the leaping flames and Elspeth's shawl weren't enough to warm me. I still shivered.

"I am also feeling the cold most particularly today," said Mrs. De Lancey.

Her usual wrap of gossamer had been replaced by a homespun woolen shawl, but she, too, was shivering.

"How is your grandmother this morning?" she asked.

"Not better," I said.

"I'm very sorry," said Mrs. De Lancey. "I know how it is to have a loved one so ill, and to fear . . ." She looked at me with what I thought of as her truest face, in which I could see real kindness and caring.

"I had Dr. Jordan stop a moment with me," she said. "A most learned and good-hearted man, indeed, a finer doctor than that society quack, Parks. Anyway, he said we must not give up our hopes for Mrs. Jones."

I never had. I never would.

"Shall I read you another chapter from Mr. Swift's *Gulliver's Travels*?"

"Yes, please," I said. These were the times I liked best with Mrs. De Lancey. I worked at my knitting or sewing while the wondrous story unfolded. Mrs. De Lancey had a beautiful voice, and she knew how to give the words just the right melody and meaning so that I could sink completely into the story.

Gulliver had troubles as great, if not greater, than my own. Yet I believed he would triumph over his adversity. Why would Mr. Swift bother to write the story if Gulliver didn't survive? I would have to believe that I could survive the smallpox, escape recapture by Mr. Thomas, and somehow find my way home — that I, too, could triumph.

13

The Thirteenth Card

"Miss Jones!" said Mrs. De Lancey, rapping on the table. "It is your turn."

I stared at the cards in my hand and could make no sense of the spots of black and red, nor the pictures of odd-looking kings and queens. Mrs. De Lancey had explained the game of piquet to me many times. Each time I understood what she told me until the lesson was over and it came time to play. Then all her explanations flew right out of my head.

Mrs. De Lancey was losing patience and so was I. I couldn't play this Devil's game, because every time I touched the pagan cards I thought how it would horrify my mother to see me thus engaged. Then I'd think about my family and miss them to the point of tears. I'd begin to worry all over again about them, whether they had survived the night of the raid. Were they, indeed, safe in Litchfield? Then I'd worry about Mr. Thomas finding us, and what the smallpox was doing to Mother Thomas. I'd written to Pruitt Jones yesterday morning. I thanked him for his warning, told him all about the smallpox, and said we *would* need his help, and I'd write again. Hitty said Moses would deliver my letter to the Sailor's Arms that afternoon when he went into town on errands for Mrs. Willows. That was all I could do for the moment, write to Pruitt Jones, worry, and watch over Mother Thomas as the disease ran its awful course.

I didn't want to play piquet. I didn't think it was in any way as diverting as Mrs. De Lancey claimed it to be. My head grew hotter and heavier each time she went over the rules of play.

"I'm sorry," I said, trying to sound contrite. "I am much too stupid to play piquet. Could we please read instead?"

"No!" said Mrs. De Lancey. "Reading has given me a headache."

"Perhaps I could read to you?"

"Thank you, no, Miss Jones." Mrs. De Lancey did little to hide her annoyance. "I want to play piquet," she said. "If only you would apply yourself a bit more, I'm sure you could master the game. Then we could have *such fun*."

I stared at the hateful playing cards while Mrs. De Lancey began explaining the rules of the game once again. No doubt I was being stubborn, and perhaps compromising my safety by not trying harder to please Mrs. De Lancey, sister-in-law to General Tryon, former Royal Governor of New York. A word from her and General Tryon could have me executed. There was so much at stake, but at the moment, I simply didn't care.

Two days had passed since Dr. Jordan's visit. Mother Thomas's condition hadn't improved. It seemed that Mrs. Willows exerted herself more than ever, concocting, brewing, sitting by Mother Thomas's side, endeavoring to get her to swallow just one more drop of broth. Morning, noon, and night she held Mother Thomas's wrist, her large body absolutely still as she felt the erratic beating of my friend's poor heart. Mrs. Willows was, as ever, calm and unruffled, but I felt there was greater urgency in all she did for Mother Thomas. I could hardly bear to look at my friend. She was so sadly changed, and in such deep misery.

Several times every day I would try to convince Hitty, and myself, that Mother Thomas would get better.

"Stranger things have happened," she'd say. "But don't depend on miracles."

That is exactly what I did. I latched on to the idea of a miracle. It seemed perfectly reasonable. Wasn't my capture and the burning of my home such bad luck, it was the opposite of a miracle? So it only made sense that I was due for a piece of *good* luck, a miracle that would save Mother Thomas and get us both to Connecticut.

"*Miss Jones!* I don't believe you've heard a word I've said!"

"No, ma'am," I said. "Please excuse me, my mind is elsewhere."

"Bother it!" said Mrs. De Lancey. With one sweep of her arm, she cleared the table of playing cards. Some landed in the hearth, burst into flames, and flew up the chimney.

I was too frightened to look at her.

"I'm sorry . . ." I began.

Mrs. De Lancey reached across the table, grabbed the remaining cards out of my hand, and threw them all into the flames. The fire blazed up briefly.

"Good riddance!" she said, and laughed. "That was most refreshing. Perhaps I should burn all my possessions."

Then she leapt up from her chair and nearly fell back again, her hands clutching her temples. I hastened to her side.

"It is nothing," she said. She put her arm around my shoulders in a quick embrace. "I only moved too suddenly for my poor, throbbing head."

She went to the wooden chest in the corner and began sorting through its contents. "I'm quite sure I told Isabella to pack them," she said. "They will be just the thing to amuse us."

Mrs. De Lancey's ideas of amusement didn't always agree with mine. Still, I was curious; she seemed so intent on this new scheme.

"Pepito," she called.

He appeared immediately. When questioned, he pointed to a high shelf across the room.

"Of course!" said Mrs. De Lancey. "How good of Isabella to remember. The Tarot must be respected and kept above other things." Pepito climbed on a chair and retrieved the box. Mrs. De Lancey brought it back to the table.

The dark wooden box smelled of spice and faraway places. On its lid were carved and gilded images of the sun and moon, surrounded by a constellation of stars. Mrs. De Lancey rested her hand upon the box.

"Herein lies the future," she said. "Do you dare to see what it holds for you?"

This sounded like more of the Devil's work — seeing into the future. An honest Christian should have nothing to do with it. And yet, if I could only see my way home in her crystal ball, or whatever it was inside the box, I was willing to look. I said yes, and instantly regretted it. If my future could be seen, wouldn't my true identity also be revealed? But it was too late. Mrs. De Lancey had already opened the box.

She took out a smaller package wrapped in black silk. As she unwrapped the silk, she spread it out and smoothed it so that it almost covered the tabletop. And there, in the middle of the table, sat another pack of playing cards! I was both relieved and angry. I'd thought she'd given up on cards. Was she merely switching to a different game? Mrs. De Lancey was too caught up with her new game to notice my displeasure.

"Now, first," she said, "I will mix the cards to wake them up." She began shuffling the deck. These cards were nearly twice the size of those we'd used for piquet, and there seemed to be many more of them. The celestial pattern on the box was repeated on the backs of the cards. The faces that flashed by as she shuffled looked like small, strange paintings, nothing at all like the piquet cards.

"Then you cut the deck away from you three times," said Mrs. De Lancey. "Do you understand?"

"Yes, ma'am." I steeled myself for the next onslaught of rules and helpful hints.

"While cutting the cards you must keep in mind your most pressing question, and your heart's desire. All right?"

I nodded and waited for further instructions.

"Well, go ahead," she said.

"That's all I have to do? There aren't any rules?"

"No rules," said Mrs. De Lancey, laughing.

As I cut the cards, I held the image of my family in my mind. My heart's desire was so simple, only to be with my family, all of us safe and sound. After I cut the cards, Mrs. De Lancey gathered up the deck. Then she laid out seven cards in a horseshoe shape, face down on the silk. She took a deep breath and looked at me.

"Ready?"

"Yes, ma'am," I said, not sure I was ready at all.

She revealed the card at the upper left of the horseshoe. It was a picture of six goblets wreathed with flowers and hearts.

"The first card is the past," said Mrs. De Lancey. "The Six of Cups shows that it was safe and happy. Your family?"

I nodded.

She revealed the next card, marked with the words, "Il Torre" and "XVI." It showed a stone tower struck by lightning, flames and smoke pouring from the ruined rooftop and windows.

"Ah, yes!" said Mrs. De Lancey. "The Tower, the sixteenth card of the Major Arcana. A very powerful symbol. Natural disaster is defining your present. That would be the smallpox, wouldn't you agree?"

I couldn't move or speak. There was my home, my once safe and solid home, in flames.

"And the fire!" said Mrs. De Lancey.

I nodded.

"Does the Tarot frighten you?" she asked.

Of course it frightened me, that a pack of cards could show my life so clearly.

"It's all right," I said. "Please continue."

Mrs. De Lancey turned the third card in the sequence. It showed a strong-looking man who carried a stout wooden club, like a broken-off tree branch. Eight other such clubs stood in a row beside him.

"The Nine of Wands is the card of your future," said Mrs. De Lancey. She peered at me. "It shows great strength, Miss Jones."

I was still staring at the Tower and wondering if the man with the branches could make it whole again. Meanwhile, Mrs. De Lancey turned the fourth card. It was a man, similar to the one before. He also carried a thick, short branch, but his was raised to ward off the blows of six attacking clubs.

"Hmm," said Mrs. De Lancey. She was silent for a moment, studying the card.

"The Seven of Wands shows that you have many obstacles which require strength and courage to overcome."

In other words, *Be brave, Hope.* I heard my father's words again, and those of Mother Thomas. They were the last words she'd said to me. Tears came.

"Oh dear," said Mrs. De Lancey. "I'd meant for this to be fun — to take our minds off our troubles. Perhaps I should stop now?"

I wiped my eyes. "Please go on, I want to know the rest."

Mrs. De Lancey sighed and turned the fifth card. It showed a beautiful woman, sitting on a throne. In one hand she held a large gold coin, and in the other a golden scepter. She wore a golden crown, tilted back slightly as she gazed off into the distance.

Mrs. De Lancey sat back and clapped her hands. "The Queen of Pentacles is your friend and guide," she said. "How clever of the cards! Do you see it?" Mrs. De Lancey turned in her chair, offering me a profile very like the queen on the Tarot card.

It did seem fitting that Mrs. De Lancey should appear in the cards. She'd come into my life so suddenly and taken me on so completely.

"Well, Miss Jones," she said. "The Tarot doesn't lie. The *Queen* of Pentacles is and *will be* your friend and patroness. And you thought I was merely *Lady* De Lancey!"

I forced myself to smile with her. But the Queen of Pentacles frightened me as much as the attacking clubs and blazing tower. Mrs. De Lancey's merriment ceased when she turned the next card.

There was a girl bound to a post, while eight swords pierced her body.

134

"What is it? What does it mean?"

"The Eight of Swords is an unfortunate card," said Mrs. De Lancey. "It shows difficulties that cannot be avoided. You must persevere and be patient."

"She's been stabbed in so many places," I said. "She'll surely die!"

"No," said Mrs. De Lancey. "She is going to survive, as are you. This card is a sign that the worst is over."

Mrs. De Lancey was working hard to be cheerful, but her bright smile didn't mask the foreboding look in her eyes.

"It's the pox, isn't it?"

"It may be the pox," she said.

"I shall get as sick as my grandmother."

"It doesn't *say* that," she said. "Trust me."

The demon cards glowed too brightly on the black silk. They hurt my eyes and my head, too.

"Well, let's see how this will end," said Mrs. De Lancey, and she upturned the last of the cards.

"No!" I cried. "Take it back!"

A bold "XIII" was printed across the top of the card — the thirteenth card. I didn't need Mrs. De Lancey to tell me what it meant. The meaning was unmistakable. A skeleton in a black cape wielded a silver scythe. At his feet were the bodies of his victims. Mrs. De Lancey was pale and silent. There was nothing for her to say. She could not soften nor obscure this card's design with her clever talk. She could not reason away Death.

There was a knock at the door. Hitty burst in, breathless.

"Miss Hope," she said. "*Come quick!*"

14

Alone

All was dark, and I was swimming. No. I was running across the Sound toward a point of light on the far shore. The light was my home. Only I couldn't run because I kept sinking into the water. I fell to my hands and knees. I pushed against the waves with my feet and pulled with my hands, digging my nails into water as thick as mud. A ticking clock measured the passing hours. I was too tired to go one more inch, but I kept on, because I had to get home!

By and by, the sea began to smell of mint and chamomile. Someone was brewing tea. The light grew brighter. I was nearly there!

I woke from my dream and opened my eyes to a place I knew but could not name. Mother's clock was on the mantel, its ticking a tiny voice in the quiet room.

A woman who looked like Grandmother Burr's servant Rachel was sitting by my bed. I knew she wasn't Rachel, but I couldn't think who she might be. She leaned over, felt my brow, and smiled.

"Welcome back," she said. Then she turned and spoke to someone else in the room. "She's awake."

"And thirsty, I'll warrant," said a large, heavy woman arriving at my side with a steaming cup.

They propped me up and spooned mint tea into my willing mouth. I was as dry as a desert. The large woman watched me drink with a look of satisfaction.

"You've been through quite an ordeal, Miss Jones," she said.

And then it came back to me. Not all of it, but enough.

Mother Thomas was dead. Mrs. De Lancey's horrid, demon cards had been right. Dr. Jordan had been right. Mrs. Willows had been right. They'd foretold death, and it had come. I hadn't wanted to believe it. I hadn't allowed myself to think it, as if I could keep Mother Thomas alive by not considering the possibility of her death. But it hadn't worked. I may have deceived myself, but not Death.

I sank back against the pillows and wept like a baby for Mother Thomas and for myself. I was not one step nearer my home. I was still so far away, and now, so alone.

"Missy Hope," cooed Hitty. "You have been so brave, do not weep now." And she coaxed a few more spoonfuls of tea into me.

That afternoon when Mrs. De Lancey's fortune-telling had been interrupted by Hitty, I had jumped up from the table, scattering the Tarot cards. I ran up the stairs, ahead of Hitty, and was in time to say good-bye to Mother Thomas. She looked at me with shining eyes, free from the clouds of her fever. She struggled to speak, just managing to breathe my name. And then, as a flame is extinguished, she was gone.

Mrs. Willows said her heart had given out. Her kind and steadfast heart didn't survive the battle with smallpox. I thought of all the difficulties she'd undertaken for my sake, and how she had persevered no matter what. She had died trying to right the wrong done by her son.

I helped Hitty bathe Mother Thomas and comb out her silver hair. That evening Mrs. Willows, Mrs. De Lancey, Hitty, Isabella, and I stitched her shroud. That night I became too sick to know or care what happened next. Now I had to face the unbearable.

Mother Thomas had kept my hope alive. In spite of our troubles, she had always insisted, and I'd believed her, that we would find a way to get to my family. I didn't see how I would manage on my own. Did I dare to buy a horse and try to find my way home alone?

Once I'd paid my debt to Mrs. Willows for our care and board, and the burial of Mother Thomas, would there be enough silver and pewter left to buy a horse? Would there be enough for my bed and board until I could find some way to leave New York? Now was the time to ask Pruitt Jones for help. But what could I ask of him? I didn't think there'd be any point in pursuing the plan of going to Mother Thomas's cousins in Bedford. Could I ask Pruitt Jones to sail me to Fairfield? But he hated the Rebels, loved the *Marianne*, and might lose her in Rebel waters. I had to find a way. I had to think of something. I had to get home.

"Miss Jones," said Mrs. Willows. "Try to drink what you can, rest, and get stronger. The worst *is* over. By the grace of God, you've survived!"

I tried to sit up but couldn't on my own. At least I had to stop sobbing. It was shameful. Hitty propped me up again and passed me a handkerchief. I had a few sips of tea and began with the simpler questions on my mind.

"What day is it?" I asked. "How long have I been sick?"

"It's Monday," said Mrs. Willows. "You've hardly been conscious since Monday last."

When Mother Thomas died.

I touched my face and felt the hardened bumps of pox scattered all over my cheeks and brow.

"Do they itch?" asked Hitty.

"No."

"I've been dabbing your face with a lotion," she said. "That has calmed the itching, but don't touch your face, or the itching will start up something fierce."

"All right," I said. I cleared my throat and steadied myself by clinging to the bedclothes.

"Where is my grandmother?"

"Buried not far from here," said Mrs. Willows. "Moses will take you there when you're feeling able."

Dead and buried amongst strangers because she'd helped me.

"Was there someone to speak for her?" I asked.

"Dr. Jordan brought Reverend Shewkirk. And a very peculiar man showed up, the one who sent your grandmother a letter by way of Dr. Jordan."

"Pruitt Jones. But how did he know?"

Mrs. Willows shrugged. "He didn't say."

I was glad Mother Thomas had one good friend to see her to her rest.

"The reverend was kindly and well spoken," Mrs. Willows continued. "I think you would have been satisfied."

"I'd like her to have a headstone," I said. I owed her so much, that was the least I could do.

"Mrs. De Lancey has already made the arrangements. The headstone is nearly finished, only waiting for whatever words you wish carved on it."

"The stone carver brought it round to show Mrs. De Lancey," said Hitty. "You'll be pleased, Miss Hope; it's a lovely angel he's carved for Mrs. Jones."

"That was kind of Mrs. De Lancey," I said. It *was* kind, so why didn't I feel grateful?

"Mrs. De Lancey has been most thoughtful," said Mrs. Willows. "Even though she was feeling poorly, she insisted on being at the graveside with Hitty and I. She said she'd be your eyes. Isabella stayed to tend you and Pepito."

"Are Mrs. De Lancey and Pepito well now?"

"Both are fine," said Mrs. Willows. "Neither one was sick more than a day or two."

"Mrs. De Lancey has sat with you morning and evening for the past four days," said Hitty, beaming. "I think you've found your guardian angel, Miss Hope."

Mrs. Willows nodded and smiled. They were both so pleased for my recovery and the friendship shown me by Mrs. De Lancey. I would have been more pleased if I were indeed Hope Jones. Hope Wakeman had far too many worries to be pleased about much of anything. But I knew I should try to look pleased. My head pounded, but I arranged a smile on my face. Then I settled back against the pillows, closed my eyes, and prayed that somehow I'd get back to my family.

When next I woke, Mrs. De Lancey was sitting at my side, reading. I was able to watch her for a minute or two, unobserved. This difficult, elegant woman had been very kind to me. I should have been more grateful. But I felt that she required something of me in return, something I could not give.

"Hello," she said, looking up from her book.

"How is Mr. Gulliver?" I asked.

"As always," she said. "He exchanges one set of difficulties for another."

Like me.

"How do you feel?" she asked.

"Better, I think."

Mrs. De Lancey smiled.

"You *look* much better," she said. "You've been so ill, neither Dr. Jordan, nor that quack, Parks, believed you'd recover. But Mrs. Willows said you'd make it through, and I put my faith in her."

"Hitty said you helped nurse me. Thank you."

"I couldn't sit by completely idle, while Hitty and Mrs. Willows tended you so unstintingly."

She sat watching me, her book in her lap.

"I was right about your strength, Miss Jones," she said. "You fought valiantly to come back to us."

"Mrs. Willows said that I wouldn't get so sick."

"Dr. Jordan said he felt that the inoculation wasn't any help to you; you'd already contracted the disease from your grandmother."

"Oh." What more was there to say?

"The important thing," said Mrs. De Lancey, "is that you have survived."

Unlike Mother Thomas. I stifled the sob I felt rising in my chest. I didn't want Mrs. De Lancey's comforting.

"Thank you for seeing to my grandmother's headstone, and for attending the burial even though you were sick."

"I wanted to assure you that everything was done properly, and it was. When you feel able, you must tell me what to have put on the headstone."

That would take some thought. Could I let Mother Thomas lie buried under a false name? Or would she have preferred Maude Jones?

"Fate has brought us together, Miss Jones, and I feel a responsibility toward you. Remember the Tarot?"

Mrs. De Lancey was quiet, watching me. I felt she was about to say something I didn't want to hear. I fingered the fine edge of the linen sheet, trying to think of something to distract her.

"May I please have something to drink?" I asked.

"Of course! Mrs. Willows said I was to get you to drink as much as possible, and I'd nearly forgotten!"

She went to the hearth, filled the teapot, brought it back to the bedside, and poured me a cup of tea. Once I was propped up and drinking the tea, she resettled herself in the chair where I had kept vigil over Mother Thomas. Mrs. De Lancey was in the chair, I was in the sickbed, and Mother Thomas was in the ground. As often as I tried to impress upon myself what had happened, I still found it hard to accept. Mrs. De Lancey cleared her throat, and I could think of nothing to stop whatever she was about to say.

"Your pox will be infectious for a week or so, but both Mrs. Willows and Dr. Jordan agree that your convalescence will take much longer."

I nodded and felt the effort of that simple movement.

"Once you are free of the pox, there's no reason for you to remain here," said Mrs. De Lancey. "And as there has been no response from your cousins, I've decided to take you to my sister's house as soon as Mrs. Willows says I may."

Now it was my turn to express gratitude for her kindness. It *was* a kindness, but it filled me with horror. I would be staying at the home of General Tryon. I would have to keep up the pretense of being a Loyalist and maintain that my family didn't exist. Under the watchful eye of Mrs. De Lancey, it would be extremely difficult to contact my family. How on earth would I get to them? I'd need shelter and care for what sounded like a long time. I doubted that I'd have enough to pay for a long convalescence. But Mrs. De Lancey's patronage could cut off whatever freedom I might have to escape from New York. Worst of all, there was no one to understand my misery. Mother Thomas was dead; I was alone.

Yet, there was no refusing Mrs. De Lancey, for, in her eyes, I was an orphan in need. What other options did I have?

I swallowed my tears and spoke. "You are very kind. I shall be most grateful."

"It will be such fun!" said Mrs. De Lancey. "I've always wanted a little girl of my own. And now, Hope, I have you!"

15
The Gilded Cage

It was weeks before I could sit up on my own, climb out of bed, and tie on my wrapper. But every day I got a tiny bit stronger. Christmas had long since passed and spring began to show itself. I watched its progress in the tree that tapped against my window. First the buds grew ruddy as the sap began to run. Then it put forth tiny clusters of lacy flowers and damp-looking wrinkled leaves.

"My silver maple," said Mrs. Tryon, "blooms before anything else. It lets us know winter is over, spring's begun."

Mrs. Tryon and Mrs. De Lancey couldn't have been nicer. Mrs. Tryon was much like her sister, only a little older, plumper, and calmer. The general was cordial in a very formal way. I didn't see much of him, and hadn't yet met Mr. De Lancey, who was with the British troops in the South.

Anything that was deemed necessary for my recovery or my comfort was instantly procured. I had my own large room. The walls were covered with a garden of flowers printed on paper come all the way from China. I slept alone in a big bed curtained with damask and net. There were sparkling looking glasses, dainty chairs, a pretty desk, and a tea table inlaid with mother-of-pearl. On the tables, shelves, and mantel above the hearth were many delicate china figurines, carved boxes of onyx or sandalwood, seashells, and other ornaments. Isabella had put Mother's clock on the mantel, and of all the pretty things, it was the only one that gave me pleasure. Everything else filled me with despair. I was so lonely for my family and Mother Thomas, but I couldn't give in to sorrow, nor give up. I had to get well, I had to get strong enough to find a way home.

I began to see that while Mrs. De Lancey and Mrs. Tryon were at home, they were constantly attentive. Mornings they came to my room in their silk wrappers to have their hair dressed by Isabella and Madame Epard, so that they might keep me company. They gossiped continuously during the tedious business of having their hair arranged. Most of their chatter was too silly to listen to, like the chirping of birds. But sometimes they spoke of the war. Then they ceased to chirp.

The war wasn't going as well as the British had expected, though the Rebels were greatly outnumbered by "superior forces." General Clinton's failure to free Burgoyne's captured army was discussed at length, while I feigned interest in my book lest my happy heart betray me.

Their hair was powdered, curled, wrapped over rats, and combined with false plaits, bows, and feathers, creating fashionably towering shapes. Then they began the equally elaborate process of dressing. Thankfully, I was still deemed too ill to be tortured in a like manner. Coiffed and dressed, the ladies went off on visits or shopping excursions for the greater part of every afternoon. There were many hours during the day when I was on my own. Mrs. De Lancey often expressed regret at leaving me alone.

"When you are fully recovered, you'll come with us everywhere," she said. "Poor darling, you must be getting so bored."

I wasn't at all bored, only worried about the days stretching into weeks and months since I had been away from my family. And the day was coming soon when I'd be taken about with Mrs. De Lancey and Mrs. Tryon and wouldn't have the least chance of managing my escape from New York.

The stronger I got, the less Isabella bothered with me, as well. Once she'd brought me dinner and seen me comfortably settled with a book for company, she'd leave me undisturbed. With careful planning, I'd be able to go out without being missed.

Before I'd left Mrs. Willow's, I'd written another letter to Pruitt Jones, telling him where I'd be and hinting that I was not yet well enough to receive visitors. What would happen if he showed up, asking his questions? What would Mrs. De Lancey think? I wished I could have given him some last message from Mother Thomas. I wished I had one myself. Death comes with such a lonesome silence.

I thought of writing to Mr. Thomas, to tell him about his mother. It seemed fitting that he should know. I also wondered if I should tell him that I'd be staying with General Tryon, and he must keep away else I'd have the general put him in irons. That plan might turn upon me, though, for what if Mr. Thomas told the general that he was harboring a Rebel's daughter? I might find *myself* in irons. In the end, I asked Pruitt Jones to tell Mr. Thomas of his mother's illness and death, and to say that I'd been taken into the household of a Westchester family. I hoped that would throw him off my trail. But I could well imagine Elspeth goading him into pursuit, no matter what, out of meanness and longing for her lost shawl and boots, not to mention my family's pewter and silver that she'd come to consider her own.

For now I had to put the Thomases out of my mind and concentrate on finding an escape from my gilded cage. To that end I'd begun to insist on getting myself fully dressed each morning. While I was spared the more elaborate toilette of Mrs. De Lancey and Mrs. Tryon, my new clothes required a lot more dressing than the simple suit Mother Thomas had given me, or the dresses I'd worn at home. I made sure I was completely dressed so that when the opportunity came I'd be ready to walk out the door. And, except for my paper-soled slippers, which would never do for the streets of New York, I was ready.

"I'm so glad you're showing an interest in your attire," said Mrs. De Lancey. "I take it as a sign of your recovery."

"It seems sinful to laze about in my shift and wrapper all day," I said.

"My little puritan!" said Mrs. De Lancey, and laughed.

I often, inexplicably, gave Mrs. De Lancey and Mrs. Tryon cause for merriment. And I was constantly perplexed by them. Both of Mrs. Tryon's children were at school in London. The servants did all the housework. There was even a servant to direct the other servants. The occupations of Mrs. De Lancey and Mrs. Tryon were limited to dressing, paying calls, and going to parties and other amusements. Occasionally Mrs. Tryon took up her embroidery. Mrs. De Lancey had Isabella work hers so that it looked as if there were some progress when she took up her needle during her Thursdays "at home." It was so different at home, where Mother was employed all day with our care, making our clothes, teaching the girls their letters, and helping us to play the spinet and sing hymns. She also worked with Martha and Nan cooking, cleaning, and mending. Grandmother Burr was just as active in her stately house, always taking part in the work despite having four servants. I couldn't understand how Mrs. De Lancey and Mrs. Tryon could lead such busy lives and do so little.

On the day in April when Mrs. De Lancey and Mrs. Tryon set out to visit the Beekmans, I was ready to try my first excursion. I was desperate to get to the postmaster to see if Mother had gotten my letter and written back. The postmaster's office was in the Sun Tavern, just a few streets away. If I took my time, I thought I could manage it. The hardest part would be getting out of the house and back in again.

The carriage left at eleven. Isabella brought my dinner before noon, then went to join the other servants in the kitchen. Before she left, I asked her not to disturb me again until teatime. I told her I'd put the tray on the landing to be collected and nap all afternoon.

"Yes, miss," she said, and quietly closed the door, as if I were already asleep.

I wrapped the bread and mince-pie in a napkin to save for later, and poured most of the soup into the slop jar. Then I put on Elspeth's boots and shawl and tiptoed down the wide stairs. Hugging the wall, I hardly saw the precipice beyond the banisters. The only problem was that by keeping close to the wall, I was obliged to walk on the slick polished wood, instead of the thick Persian runner going down the center of the stairs. I could easily slip, hurtle down the steps, and be dashed against the black-and-white flagged floor of the hall. I stopped on the first landing to catch my breath and listened for the servants. All I heard was the ticking of the tall clock. I slipped past its watchful face and out the front door.

It was a shock to be outside. I'd been so long abed, and longer still confined indoors. Even careful observation of the silver maple hadn't prepared me for the glorious sensation of being in the fresh air. The day was clear, with a stiff breeze blowing off the water. The chill wind and warm sun on my face were so welcome. I had to pinch myself to move along and not stand loitering on the front steps for all to see. I looked about me, lest Mr. Thomas lay in wait, then I made my slow way, on wobbly legs, down the street, away from the imposing house that fronted on the harbor. Used to the peace and quiet of my back room, I found the clatter and shouts of the streets deafening. I started at the harsh noises of every passing carriage and dray. The *stomp, stomp, stomp* of a column of Redcoats sent me scurrying into the refuge of a milliner's shop.

"May I help you, miss?"

"Thank you, no," I squeaked.

The clerk looked puzzled. I had to give some reason for my presence. "Could you please direct me to the postmaster's office?" I asked.

"Two streets up on the right, in the Sun Tavern," he said. "You can't miss it. There's a rising sun painted on the signboard with real gold. 'Tis brighter than the day itself."

"Thank you, sir," I said, and left the safety of the shop. The tumult of the streets had unnerved me, but I had to get hold of myself else I'd never make it to the postmaster and back.

I continued up Broad Street, and having achieved the first corner, my legs were ready to give out. It was only a few more yards to the Sun Tavern. The sign was gleaming just ahead. Yet I didn't know if I could force myself to complete that short distance.

If not forward, then what? It was the same distance back to the general's house, and each step I'd gained would be wasted. I stood on the corner, gulping the spring air.

Go on, Hope, I admonished myself. *Mother's letter may be waiting for you!* That thought propelled me across the street, and I managed all the slow, painful steps up to the Sun Tavern. I crossed the threshold and sank into a chair by the door. I stayed there until my head stopped spinning and I'd regained some strength in my legs. The tavern maid offered me a drink of water, which I gladly accepted. Finally, I stood and slowly advanced to the postmaster's office, in a small alcove off the main room. Behind his wide desk was a wall of cubbyholes, at least one for each letter of the alphabet. I could see several letters in the "W" box, and my heart began to race.

I had to wait my turn while an old gentleman wrangled over the cost of sending a letter to Philadelphia. In the end, he decided it wasn't worth it.

"What can I do for you?" asked the postmaster, leaning over his desk with an encouraging smile.

"I'm hoping for a letter, sir." My voice was that of a stranger's it was so weak and pitiful. Until that moment I hadn't let myself know how hungry I was for that letter.

"Name?"

"Hope Wakeman." It was a joy to say those two words out loud, to reclaim myself for one moment.

He scooped up the letters from the "W" box, studied each one, and turned to me.

"Sorry," he said. "Not today."

Nothing. Not a single word to hope on.

"Are you sure?"

"Quite sure. Where would your letter be coming from?"

"Litchfield, Connecticut."

"Very little comes in from Connecticut," he said. "It's Rebel territory, you know."

"Yes, sir." I knew it all too well.

He took off his spectacles and peered at me. "Weren't you here in the early winter, with a handsome older lady, sending a letter to Litchfield?"

"Yes, sir."

"Perhaps your letter was never received. I remember telling you that letters across the Rebel borders were an uncertainty."

I nodded.

"Perhaps you should write again," he said. "You mustn't give up."

A sob had started in my chest and was pushing its way up my throat. I had to leave immediately. I bowed and walked to the door as quickly as I could make my legs carry me.

I knew it was too much to expect a letter from Mother, but I had hoped. I'd dreamed that it would be, and it wasn't.

I barely made it back to the Tryons' house,

the weight of my disappointment so great, and my strength so limited. I got into the house un-observed, crawled up the stairs, and fell into bed. I mustn't give up, not now. Somehow, I'd find a way home.

16

Friend or Foe?

I took a chill while going to the postmaster and was back in bed for another month. During that time the silver maple at my window came into full leaf. When Isabella threw open the windows, some of the silver-bellied leaves poked into my room. It was mid-May before I was feeling better, but I kept my recovered health to myself.

"If it weren't for the stubborn Colonials, and this stupid war, I'd take you away from this dirty place," said Mrs. De Lancey. "Though I can't imagine why you sickened when you've been kept safely indoors."

I chose that moment to sneeze.

"God bless," said Mrs. De Lancey. "Really, Hope, we can't have any fun until you are completely well. Maybe I should have Parks in to bleed you."

I wondered if Mrs. De Lancey regretted taking me in. I wasn't proving to be very amusing after all. I was actually feeling well, but feigned continued illness to avoid the "fun" Mrs. De Lancey had in mind for me. During the past weeks I'd composed another letter to Mother, and one to my best friend, Prudence Perry, in case letters to Fairfield had a better chance of getting through than those to Litchfield. Before Mrs. De Lancey caught me up in her round of social calls and entertainments, I was determined to go to the post-master again. I would send my letters and look for one from home. As the kind man had said, I "mustn't give up."

My chief errand was to deliver a letter for Pruitt Jones at the Sailor's Arms. I had decided that my only hope of getting to Connecticut was on a horse of my own. As Mrs. De Lancey had generously paid all of my debts to Mrs. Willows, I was left with most of my family's pewter and silver, and the remaining silver in Mother Thomas's purse. I would spend it all, if necessary, on a reliable mount. To this end I was asking Captain Jones for help. No doubt a man, even an odd one like Pruitt Jones, would have more success in horse dealing than I. I wrote him that as kind as Mrs. De Lancey was to me, I wanted to be with family. I shamelessly said that Mother Thomas's cousins in Bedford were my destination. This was such a familiar lie, it was easy to sustain. I told Pruitt Jones how Mother Thomas and I had tried, without luck, to hire a carriage, and that I truly felt I'd only get there on a horse of my own. I wrote down all the pretty lies and implored his help, as a noble deed in memory of our mutual friend, Maude Thomas. If I ever got back to Connecticut, I'd have many falsehoods and deceptions to atone for.

It was hard to contain my delight when Mrs. De Lancey announced that she and Mrs. Tryon would be going to Haarlem the following day. As the general was away for several days, they'd planned this longer outing. The ladies would leave early in the morning and not return until after dark.

"Naturally, we won't go if you'll feel too lonely," said Mrs. Tryon.

"Fiddlesticks!" said Mrs. De Lancey. "Hope will do nicely on her own. Isabella and Pepito will see to her every need."

"But Isabella and Pepito aren't much company in English," said Mrs. Tryon.

"I'll be fine," I said. "I shall read and have a good rest."

"And next time you'll come, too. Won't you, my dear?" said Mrs. De Lancey.

"If it is meant to be," I said, trying to look pale.

"For heaven's sake, Hope, show a little spunk," said Mrs. De Lancey. "At times I think you don't *want* to get well."

I waited until the servants were at their dinner, and was able to leave the house unnoticed again. I stood on the front steps, enchanted by the feel of hot sun and mild air. I glanced about, as I had before, lest Mr. Thomas was waiting to apprehend me, and saw no dark figure.

I set off briskly for the postmaster's office and this time my legs obeyed me. I had been secretly exercising every day in my room, walking round and round, like an ox turning a grindstone. My efforts had been worthwhile as now I marched along the street feeling strong and well. The day was brilliant, the few trees on the streets were newly dressed in their most becoming shades of spring green. Flowers bloomed in window boxes and small garden plots. I hardly minded the noises of the streets, for everything seemed lovely, easy, and safe. I felt the day itself would bring me luck, until a hand reached out from the shadow of a doorway and clamped down on my shoulder.

"I thought the sun might bring ye out."

It was Pruitt Jones!

"Still looking a might peaked."

No doubt I was white as a sheet, he'd given me such a start.

"I've been watching out for you the past few days, figured you had to come out sometime."

"I'm very glad to see you, Captain Jones," I said, once my heart had resumed beating properly. "In fact I was going to leave a letter for you at the Sailor's Arms." Now I couldn't go on to the postmaster's. Pruitt Jones would probably accompany me, then he'd see my letters to Rebel Connecticut.

"The Sailor's Arms is in the other direction," he said.

"Of course it is. I've gotten myself all turned around. I'm still not quite recovered."

"So I see," he said.

I felt more and more flustered, for it seemed as if Pruitt Jones saw entirely *too* well. There was nothing for it but to blunder on. "I've written to ask your help in purchasing a horse."

"A horse! Why ever would you be wanting a horse, when General Tryon has a whole stable full of them, a whole army of horses at his command?"

"I want a horse of my own. I want to ride to Bedford."

"Are ye running away again, girl?"

He made it sound as if I were an indentured servant breaking my bond.

"I'm just trying to get to my family," I said.

"A girl riding alone through Westchester? Even in peacetime it's a mad notion." He spat on the ground. "Must be Elspeth's bad blood."

"But there's no other way," I said. "Mother Thomas and I tried hiring a carriage, a farm wagon, anything . . ."

"Why are ye going anywhere in the first place?" His

voice rose. "What kind of girl would go tramping through the world alone? What's wrong with living in the general's mansion? Not fine enough for ye? Seems to me you've done all right for an orphan!" His last sentence came out like thunder, filled with ire and indignation. I was feeling pretty indignant myself, and mad enough to spit. How dare he judge me!

"You don't understand," I shouted. "I'm not an orphan!"

"You're right," he said calmly. "I don't understand, you'd better tell me."

He'd riled me on purpose, and I'd revealed more than ever I meant to.

"I know you haven't done anything wrong," he said. "Else Maude Thomas wouldn't have been helping you. But there is a story, isn't there, missy?"

I nodded. Should I tell him? Or should I run back to General Tryon's house and hide? Pruitt Jones hated the Patriots. But he didn't hate me. And he'd loved Mother Thomas.

"My name is Hope Wakeman," I said with a lump of terror in my chest. "I'm a Patriot."

Pruitt Jones glared at me but held his tongue, and I continued.

"Noah Thomas and some others burned down my home in Fairfield, Connecticut, and took me from my mother."

"What's the use of stealing a girl?" he asked.

"They'd come to capture my father, captain in the Continental army. But he was already gone to General Washington's camp."

"So that half-wit Noah took you instead?"

I nodded.

"Foolish business, and foul too. Noah Thomas, no better than a pirate! Poor Maude, it must have broken her heart."

"Elspeth was going to sell me to the Hunting Town trader."

"Well, that sounds like Elspeth." Pruitt Jones sighed and scratched his white whiskers. "So you're a Rebel brat?"

I stood up straight and looked him square in the eye. "Yes, sir, I am."

"And you're living with General Tryon, former Royal Governor of New York!" Pruitt Jones slapped his thigh and roared. "Ha, ha, ha!"

"It isn't all that funny," I said.

He stopped laughing and tears filled his eyes. "No, not so funny. Not for you, and not for Maude."

"Will you help me?"

"Help a Rebel! I'll be damned if I . . ." He stopped and glowered at me. Then he took out a shred of handkerchief, blew his nose, and wiped his eyes. He scratched his whiskers some more, all the while glaring at me.

I kept still, counted my heartbeats, and tried to breathe. If I have to, I can do it without him, I thought. I don't have to depend on Pruitt Jones. And yet, I hoped with all my heart he would say yes.

"Yes," said Pruitt Jones. "I'll be damned, but I'll help you anyway."

17

Guardian Angels

"So you'll help me buy a horse?" I asked.

"You've a mickle of courage, and not a whit of sense," said Pruitt Jones.

"But I have to get home, and I don't think there's any other way. I know I haven't enough money to buy a wagon . . ."

"Didn't I say there's no going anywhere by land?" he growled. "Fairfield in Connecticut, I been there aplenty before the war. I'll take ye aboard the *Marianne*. Lord knows I hate to sail her in Rebel waters. Ah, well," he sighed. "Can't be helped."

We had moved down the street and were sitting on a bench at the harbor. Before us were the great British warships, anchored in the deeper water, and close at hand the smaller vessels that lined the quay. The *Mari-*

anne must have been in her usual slip, hidden from our vantage point. Pruitt Jones sighed again, looking out to sea.

Pruitt Jones had reason to fear taking his boat to the Connecticut shore. Piracy was rampant, and there were Rebel patrols. The *Marianne* would be at risk, and the *Marianne* was all Pruitt Jones had in the world. I didn't want him to lose his boat in helping me. It was bad enough, all that Mother Thomas had suffered on my account. No one needed further trouble. I looked out at all the boats bobbing gently on their lines. Then I had a thought.

"The night Mr. Thomas and his men took me, they also stole my father's dory, the *Liberty*. Percy, Dimon, and Brewster took charge of it. Do you know them?"

Pruitt Jones spat again.

"Aye, I know them," he said.

"What if we took back my father's boat?"

"Ha!" shouted Pruitt Jones. "That's a plan. So you're clever as well as courageous!"

"I'm not brave."

"No?"

"No."

"I'd say you and Maude were brave enough, walking out of Noah's house in the dead of night and traipsing all around New York Town without a friend's protection. Hmph! You and Maude! One day I had to follow you halfway to Greenwich Village."

"You followed us?"

"Someone had to look out for you," said Pruitt Jones. "But I couldn't protect ye from the pox."

"You've been following us all over New York?"

"And you never noticed, did you?" Pruitt Jones was looking pleased as rum punch. "I think Maude knew. No good trying to fool her."

"But why didn't you say something?" I asked.

"I figured Maude had her reasons for not telling me her business. Maybe she was ashamed about Noah. Anyway, I didn't want to interfere, only to be there in case of trouble."

It took some getting used to, Pruitt Jones as a guardian angel, *my* guardian angel. Of course mostly he was looking out for Mother Thomas. But here he was sitting by my side, although now he was looking at me as sour as pickled onions.

"Have ye thought of this, clever girl? Once I sail you across to Fairfield and return your father's boat, how will I get back to Long Island? I cannot walk on the water, now, can I?"

My cheeks were burning because I hadn't yet thought about getting Pruitt Jones safely home.

"I don't want to be stuck in a Rebel hole the rest of this blasted war."

"My family will see that you get back," I said. "If neither my father nor uncle is there to help you, I will take you to General Silliman, in Fairfield, and tell my story. He is the commander of the militia in Fairfield, and my father's friend. He will get you back to Long Island if no one else can."

Pruitt Jones kept looking at me with cold blue eyes. I couldn't tell if he believed a word I'd said.

"You'll have to trust me," I said. "As I trust you."

"Oh, well." Solemnly he offered me his hand, and I took it. "I suppose trust is the heart of the matter, isn't it? Well, let's get on with the plan," said Pruitt Jones, brusque again.

"Do you know where the men will have tied up my father's boat?"

"Aye. Brewster's got a little cove, spitting distance from his house. He'll be keeping his pirate's gain there. A nasty lot you've been mixed up with, Miss Wakeman."

"I didn't have much choice in the matter."

"I reckon not." Pruitt Jones lost some of his cantankerous bluster. "It's all bad business." He shook his head. "Stealing a man's boat!"

Not to mention his daughter.

"So when can we get my father's boat?"

"We?"

"You'll need me to help you."

Pruitt Jones snorted. "What can you do?"

I shrugged.

"Can you sail the dory on your own?"

"No."

"Can you fire a pistol into a man's belly?"

I shook my head.

"Then you stay put 'til I come back for you."

"I could be a lookout, or something . . ." I started to protest.

"A sickly girl, you'll only be in the way." He stopped and cleared his throat. "And a worry to me."

"All right," I said. "When?"

He scratched his whiskers and studied the mare's-tail wisps across the sky. Was he reading in them the wind's force and direction? And what of the tides? How would they affect this undertaking?

"Can you be at the harbor, by the Sailor's Arms, at sunup?" he asked.

I nodded. I would be anywhere, at any time he told me.

"I'll see you then." He got up and stretched.

I stood up and my knees buckled. Pruitt Jones caught my elbow just in time to save me from a fall.

"Do you think you can make it on your own tomorrow morning?" he asked.

"Yes, thank you," I said. I would be there no matter how my body betrayed me.

"I'd better see you back to the general's house."

"I think I'd better go on alone," I said. "I'll have to get back in without being noticed."

"Just see you don't go collapsing in the street," he said, and stood, scowling, as I made my way back to General Tryon's house.

I might have been walking along like any sober citizen, but inside I was skipping and pirouetting up the street. Not another month, not another week — only this day and night separated me from the Connecticut shore. Once in Fairfield I'd know the fate of my family. I'd grown used to the idea that they would be in Litchfield with Grandmother Burr, but they could be in Fairfield! And if I had to travel on to Litchfield, perhaps the Perrys or some other friend or neighbor would help me get there. If I closed my eyes, I could remember the feel of Mother's arms, and her smell of lavender and baked apples. Soon, I'd be in her arms with my eyes wide open!

Edward, the footman, seemed to be guarding the large front door. Perhaps someone was expected for the general. I headed to the back door, where the servants came and went all day. As I came around the side of the house, I stopped to listen if anyone was coming toward me. All was quiet, so I went quickly forward. At the door, I stopped again to peek in the window and listen for sounds of activity inside. Nothing. I rushed through the door and up the back staircase to my room.

I flung open my door, ready to fall upon my bed, but instead nearly fell upon Isabella!

"Miss Jones! Where have you been?" Isabella radiated hot fury. "I worried. Mrs. De Lancey be very, very angry you go out alone!"

"I . . . , I — " I was caught. I was speechless.

"No good, young girl on street alone." Isabella's hands scolded, too. They seemed to draw pictures in the air of my bad behavior. I stood by, watching Isabella's hands dart and point, unable to think of any excuses. There were none I'd dare share with Isabella.

"I'm sorry," I managed at last. "I'm sorry I worried you."

That sent Isabella into an outburst in galloping Portuguese, which invoked "Mrs. De Lancey" several times. Then she slowed down to silence, and her hands came to rest on her hips. But she wasn't through with me yet.

"I think and Mrs. De Lancey think you too sick go out, but you go out." Her black eyes studied me, searching for secrets.

"I wanted to practice, to surprise Mrs. De Lancey with my progress."

Isabella didn't believe me, not by the way she was looking at me.

"Now I watch you," she said, pointing to her eyes and turning the finger toward me so there could be no confusion about her intent. "Pepito watch, too. You no go out alone again!"

"I won't go out again," I said. "I promise."

"Hmph!" said Isabella. She picked up my dinner tray and sailed out of the room before I could think of any way to get her to leave off her vigilance. If she and Pepito were watching, how would I ever get out of the house to meet Pruitt Jones tomorrow morning?

18
Leap of Faith

Mrs. De Lancey and Mrs. Tryon didn't return from their visit to Haarlem until long after dark. I heard the carriage pull up to the house, and then the trill of their voices in the hall and coming up the stairs. The door of my room opened. There was the swish and rustle of silk gowns. Mrs. De Lancey leaned over me, her scent engulfing me. I feigned sleep.

"Sweet dreams, Hope," she said, then murmured something to Mrs. Tryon. They both giggled, then swept out of the room. Their scent remained, heavy in the air.

Isabella greeted the ladies just outside my door. I listened to her cascade of Portuguese, every muscle in my body taut. But not once in her musical outpouring did I hear my name mentioned. Thank god! A reprieve! She didn't tell Mrs. De Lancey that I'd gone out alone. She probably kept my secret because, although it was my doing, Isabella would get the blame. I must add something to my letter about the kindness of Isabella. Something to deflect Mrs. De Lancey's anger at my departure.

I had agonized over my letter to Mrs. De Lancey. I owed her so much, but I could not feel a proper sense of gratitude, nor could I express it. I told her briefly what had happened to me, leaving out all names and places. I didn't want to have to worry about General Tryon coming after me. I said that I hadn't meant to deceive her any more than I'd meant to be kidnapped in the first place. I thanked her for her care and all the pretty things she'd bought me, none of which I was taking with me. I hoped she would find another girl to adopt, a real orphan. I was able to sincerely thank Mrs. De Lancey for all that she had done for Mother Thomas. In her tenderness toward my friend, she had won my true gratitude.

I set aside some of my family's things to pay, in part, for what Mrs. De Lancey had done for me. I felt my parents would want me to discharge my debts. I chose to leave the heaviest pieces of pewter to help lighten my burdens. It would be a long walk to the Sailor's Arms, and I had too much to carry. The canvas sacks were packed. Mother's china clock was wrapped in linen and safely stowed with Jonathan's porringer. The letter to Mrs. De Lancey was nearly finished upon the desk. I was dressed, except for my boots. Now all I had to do was figure out a way to escape Isabella's and Pepito's watchful eyes. How *was* I going to get out of the house? I still didn't know, and I'd been thinking of nothing else since Isabella had left my room that afternoon.

I did know that I *had* to go. This was my chance. I could not, would not, miss it. Only I didn't know how. It was a bad sign that Isabella had been just outside my door to intercept Mrs. De Lancey. She couldn't be planning on staying there all night long. Could she? Maybe I should make a run for it now, while Isabella was busy waiting on the ladies. No. There was too much coming and going on the stairs and in the hall. If Isabella didn't catch me leaving, someone else surely would.

The bustle of the ladies' homecoming died down. The parade of servants outside my door, bringing tea, a light supper, hot water in basins, was finally over. The house was quiet. I waited until I felt sure the ladies were abed. Then I waited some more.

I got out of bed and tiptoed to the door to listen, and see what could be seen from the keyhole. There was the sound of steady, rhythmic breathing; someone was sleeping outside my door! Whoever it was seemed deep asleep. I risked opening the door a crack. I had to know who was out there. It was Pepito, lying across the threshold, his arm for a pillow and not a scrap of blanket to cover him. I eased shut the door and crept back to my bed to think. I couldn't get past him without waking him, especially while carrying the canvas satchels and Mother Thomas's leather grip.

What if I woke him purposely? Offered him silver to let me go? Offered to take him with me? But I couldn't make Pepito understand anything in English. Even if I could, I didn't think he'd risk Isabella's heavy hand, or Mrs. De Lancey's wrath, to help me. I sat on my bed, wringing a pillow, and thought.

"Out of my distress I called on the Lord; the Lord answered and set me free."

That was a psalm our minister in Fairfield often recited. If only the angel of the Lord would come and fly me away from here. "Help!" I whispered. I could not cry out loud. Would the Lord hear me anyway? I went to the open window, and holding firmly to the sill, spoke softly to the heavens. *"Help!"*

And the Lord sent me an answer, only it wasn't what I'd hoped for. My answer was the *open window*.

I forced myself to look down. Beyond the leaves of my silver maple, the back garden was lit by a gibbous moon. I guessed it wasn't too far to the ground, *for someone who wasn't afraid of heights*. To me it looked like an endless void. I leaned back from the window and caught

177

my breath. I couldn't possibly jump. But how could I climb down? I peeked out the window, feeling the familiar heave and twist of my stomach. Without looking further, I dropped to my hands and knees and crawled back to the door. Perhaps Pepito had gone away. Perhaps I'd imagined him sleeping by the door. But Pepito was still there and I could not wish him away. There was only the window.

First I had to find a way to lower the bags to the ground, and then follow after them. As the following-after-them part made me too sick and dizzy to think, I concentrated on lowering the bags.

Mrs. De Lancey had gotten me a quantity of satin ribbons in all the pearly colors of spring, for sashes to go with the pretty new dresses. I set to work, knotting them together until I had a length I judged to be twice the distance from my window to the ground. The ribbon rope couldn't bear the weight of all three bags, and neither could I. I'd lower them one at a time, retrieving the rope once each bag was safely on the ground.

I threaded the ribbon rope through the handles of the lightest satchel, tying the two loose ends around the leg of the heavy table I'd pushed next to the window. I eased the satchel off the ledge. I backed away from the window, feeling too dizzy to watch its descent. Slowly I let out the lengths of knotted ribbon, thinking with every knot that slipped through my hands that the bag must surely be about to land. But I let out all the ribbon, and still felt the weight of the satchel suspended in air. I must have been a great deal higher than I'd thought. It was a sickening realization.

I made sure the knot was secure on the table leg and went to get more ribbons. There were only three left — nine, maybe ten more feet of rope. What if that wasn't enough?

I tied the three ribbons together, undid the rope around the table leg, and attached the new length. Adding the new ribbons meant I had to slide the satchel into a new position. It was awkward getting the handles over the rope's knots, especially as I was two stories above and unable to see what I was doing. When I'd again let out all the ribbon, the bag remained suspended in midair. Nothing had changed. I had to find out how far it was from the ground, although it meant leaning out the window to look.

I edged toward the window with eyes averted and grasped the windowsill.

"Look, Hope," I commanded my quavering self. "It is only a little thing to look down."

It *was* only a little thing; ahead of me was the much bigger thing of getting myself down. How ever would I find the courage to do that? Pruitt Jones had said I was brave. What if he could see me now, trembling at a window? I wasn't brave; not when Mother Thomas and

I had run away from Oyster Bay, not when we'd tramped about New York, and not when Mother Thomas got the smallpox. I had been frightened every single minute. I was nothing but a miserable coward: afraid of the dogs, afraid of Elspeth and Mr. Thomas. In New York, I was afraid of the soldiers and sailors, even the pigs in the streets.

I was becoming disgusted with my sniveling cowardly self. I stood, frozen at the window, filled with rage and hesitation. Then it came to me. My fears didn't matter!

Even though I'd been afraid, I'd still gone up and down that wretched ladder. I'd walked past those two vicious dogs, and I'd nursed Mother Thomas. Somehow I'd managed to do what I had to do, in spite of my fears. And *somehow*, tonight I would do what I had to do to escape the Tryon's house. Perhaps *that* was courage. The idea made me grin. Doing what had to be done, no matter how it terrified me.

I took a deep breath, leaned against the windowsill, looked down, and nearly burst out laughing. The bag was suspended only inches from the ground. I leaned out a bit more and brought the bag to rest on the ground below.

Soon all the bags lay in a silent heap beneath my window. I took the ribbon rope back to my bed. While I untied the knots and smoothed the ribbons, I considered the next part of my escape, the hard part — getting myself down. I listened for the chimes of the hall clock. How much time was there until daybreak? Should I leave as quickly as possible, or wait? Waiting would only give me more time to worry. I had to leave as soon as I could.

The moonlight that filtered through the leaves of the silver maple fell in oddly shaped patches on the floor. A gentle wind stirred the leaves and rearranged the pattern of light and dark. I finished winding the ribbons into neat rolls and tucked them back in the drawer of the dressing table.

I returned to the window. A stout branch of the maple hung below and slightly to the right of my window. It might be possible to reach if I were actually sitting on the ledge. The thought made my stomach lurch and started a quaking in the pit of my stomach that traveled outward to my arms and legs. Well, go ahead and vomit, I thought, if it will make you feel better. For though I was caught in the clenched fist of my worst fear, I was no longer frightened of being afraid.

I climbed out and sat on the ledge in an *impossible* position. My hands held fast to the ledge, my back was adhered to the window frame, but my feet were dangling in the air, an eternity above the solid ground. I was so scared and dizzy, it felt as if I were floating above myself. Everything looked so bright and terribly clear — the entire garden, and I, too, seemed delineated with light. The tree limb I had to reach was only an arm's length away. The leaves on its branches fluttered, showing their pale undersides. Beckoning me? There seemed to be plenty of branches evenly spaced around the tree, for footholds going down. Once I let go of the window ledge and got hold of the branch, the descent wouldn't be so hard.

But first I had to get to the tree. I had to *let go*.

My ears were full of the sound of my own heart. "Let go," I whispered, and my hands, the hands of the terrified girl on the ledge, obeyed. In one swift moment, I sailed through the air and caught the tree branch!

I made it! I was free!

19

Strange Bedfellow

I was stunned to find myself completely whole at the foot of the tree. My stockings were torn, my chin was bleeding, but I wasn't dead. Not even a bone was broken. I couldn't get over it. This would be such a fine tale to tell my father. I could well imagine his amazement.

"Hope," he'd say. "Can it be true? *You* jumped out a window and climbed down a tree in the dead of night to get home to us?"

I'd nod and smile. And he would take me in his arms, and I would be safe again.

But my father's embrace was still a long way off. What if my father wasn't waiting at the end of my journey? Most likely he would still be away somewhere, fighting. There were other possibilities, too. Worse ones. Ones I couldn't, wouldn't think about now. Now

I had to concentrate on getting as far away from General Tryon's house as I could as quickly as possible.

I picked up my bags. Swiftly, silently I raced around the side of the house to the street. And there I stopped abruptly, turned away from the moonlit street, went back to the deep shadow of the house, and set down my bags.

I had no idea what to do or where to go next. It must be too early by hours to meet Pruitt Jones. To wait for him on the docks 'til morning was unthinkable. The Sailor's Arms might offer shelter, but it would be boarded up for the night. I could not wander the streets. As Isabella would say, "A girl alone — no good!" Even if I escaped carousing soldiers, I might be stopped by a constable on his midnight rounds. How should I then explain myself? I'd look like a runaway servant stealing her mistress's silver.

This was the trouble with being too afraid of one thing. I hadn't been able to look beyond getting out of the window to see the problems ahead. Still, I couldn't linger on the steps of General Tryon's house. There had to be someplace between here and the harbor where I could shelter and possibly rest until daybreak. *Think*, Hope.

What was the Lord's answer for this predicament? I wondered if it would involve another tree climb. No. The answer *was* in the Lord's grace. I'd go where He would protect me, I'd go to the nearest churchyard and wait for the dawn. Toward the wharves, only a few streets away, was the Old Dutch Church. I picked up my bags, made sure the street was empty, and headed warily in that direction.

Walking the streets of the midnight town was eerie. I was increasingly conscious of my lone figure. As frightening as it had been escaping from Oyster Bay, I'd had Mother Thomas by my side. I missed her in this moment more than ever. The buildings which I'd passed without a thought only yesterday now watched me with the malevolent eyes of their unlit windows. Maybe houses at night were given over to evil spirits. The dark shadows of the doorways could be hiding anyone, or any monstrous thing. I shuddered, and marched along more quickly. A dog barked in a nearby yard, and I jumped in my skin and dropped one of the satchels. Fortunately not the one with Mother's clock in it. I was letting my fears get out of hand. I had to calm down, or I'd have no wits about me should I come across a *real danger*. So I tried to stifle my imagination and keep a sharp eye. There was plenty to worry about without inventing troubles.

The churchyard was to the right side of the old stone church, fenced round with a low wall. I clambered over the wall and made for the darkest corner. I mustn't let myself get spooked by the churchyard, even if it was filled with dead people. What if there was a restless spirit here, an unhappy ghost? Perhaps there was someone who'd been murdered and took revenge on innocent souls like me. *Stop it, Hope!* I was giving myself the shivers based on my own nonsense. I set down my bags in the shadow of a tall headstone and sank heavily to the ground beside them.

My jitters left me with a sigh. I was *so* tired. I'd been out much of the day and awake and busy all this night. It was too much after all the weeks, months, of illness, and the quiet isolation of my room. I felt as worn out and lifeless as the lumpish bags next to me. How many hours 'til morning? I was so tired, but I dared not sleep. What if I slept past dawn? I pulled Elspeth's shawl tightly around my shoulders against the cold damp of the churchyard.

I began to conjure the faces of my family one by one. That would pass the time and keep me from feeling so alone. I thought of Mary and Abigail, dressed in their Sunday best, their hair plaited and tied with matching blue ribbons. They could be such sweet sisters when they tried, and when I wasn't being too bossy with them.

I imagined holding little Jonathan, feeling his tiny hand curl with surprising strength around my finger. He wouldn't be so small anymore. I'd been gone almost seven months. He should be a big, bonny babe by now, scuttling around the kitchen floor. Maybe he was already pulling himself up, using Mother's footstool to stand.

Suddenly, hot tears were coursing down my face. Jonathan couldn't use Mother's footstool, because it had perished in the fire with everything else. I couldn't know, nor imagine what Jonathan was doing. I'd missed all the sweet months of his growing and I could never have them back. He probably wouldn't even know who I was. I lay full-length on the damp ground and sobbed, the pain in my heart growing greater. What if Jonathan hadn't grown? What if he didn't survive the night of the raid? Babies were fragile anyway, Jonathan more than most. All the worries and fears for my family came pouring out of me in a torrent of tears. What of Mother? What of Father? And Nan and Martha, were they all right? Anything could have happened to any of my dear ones while I was gone. Who would be waiting at the end of my journey? Would I return only to find more sorrow? For the first time since I'd been taken from my home, I could give full vent to my grief. There was no fear of disturbing anyone here, but I was wrong.

Through my own noisy tears, I heard the sound of someone else sniffling. I sat up stiff and still as the headstones around me, my sobs choked within me. My eyes searched the moonlight and shadows of the graves around me while my heart pounded fiercely. I could see nothing. But the soft snuffling, sniffling sound persisted. Was someone else hiding in the churchyard and crying? I didn't move. I hardly breathed; I was so concentrated on that sound. It seemed to be getting closer. Whoever it was, was near. Then, out of the silvered shadows trotted a pig. Not a monstrous sow, nor a mean-tusked boar, it was only a sweet little piglet.

"Here, pig," I said, and held out my hand.

He came right up to me and nuzzled my fingers. I patted his solid back and scratched his fine bristles.

"Good pig."

The pig grunted and plopped down beside me, sighing contentedly.

So passed the remains of the night. The pig was good company. He kept me warm, kept me from feeling too sad or too alone. Eventually the shadows grew less distinct and the sky began to pale. I heard hurrying footsteps, perhaps a servant sent to fetch water from the corner pump. A carriage passed by. It was time to leave my nest. I gently pushed the pig off my lap and stood unsteadily. I shook out my damp skirts and shawl, brushing away bits of grass and dirt. I resettled my bonnet and tied it firmly in place.

"Good-bye, pig," I said softly. "I wish I could take you with me."

The pig looked up at me, his little eyes glinting. Then he snorted and walked around the corner of the church and out of sight. I picked up my bags and went in the other direction to the street.

When I was sure no one was around to see me, I climbed back over the wall and proceeded as quickly as my wooden legs would carry me toward the harbor. Well I knew the way, but my eyes were dry and scratchy, and the streets looked strange in the predawn gloom. I stumbled along, befogged by weariness, straining to see familiar signs.

Only a few people were on the streets, but enough so that I didn't stand out too much. At least no one seemed to pay me any mind. I moved forward one heavy step after another, and it seemed as if I hardly moved at all. It was like the awful dream I'd had when I was sick, of crossing the Sound on my hands and knees. What if I got to the dock and the *Liberty* wasn't there? It would be just like my dream. I could struggle with all my might and *never* get home. The bags were unbearably heavy. I dragged as much as carried them along, and prayed that Mother's clock would survive. Step after step. One street gained and then another.

Finally my nightmarish trek came to an end. Ahead of me was the Sailor's Arms. Docked in front of it was the *Liberty*, with Pruitt Jones standing by her, readying to cast off.

"Ahoy!" he called.

My eyes cleared, my legs grew light, my arms grew strong. A few swift steps and I was at his side.

"It's about time," he said, scowling. "Too lazy to leave your soft bed?"

20

Pirates

We cast off among a number of small fishing vessels going out on their daily run with the tide. Most headed into New York Bay in the direction of Staten Island. Only the *Liberty* threaded its way through the crowded harbor going up the East River. *Liberty*, writ in gold letters on her prow, was hidden under an ugly splash of something black, paint, or perhaps tar. Brewster or Percy had done us a good turn. Better to be in an unnamed, blemished boat while in Loyalist waters than a vessel called the *Liberty*.

Pruitt Jones occasionally barked an order at me. For a short time he had me hold the tiller while he saw to a problem with the rigging. Mostly he handled the *Liberty* on his own. I made it my business to keep as much out of his way as possible. Leaving New York reminded me of the day Mother Thomas and I arrived. How the Redcoats had frightened me. They still did. But I survived the enemy city. I survived the pox. And finally I was on my way home. Although that is what I'd thought last winter when Mother Thomas and I arrived in New York. There were still many things that could keep me from my home, ill winds, shipwreck . . .

"Corlear's Hook," said Pruitt Jones as we rounded the bump of land jutting into the East River. The sun was just coming up as we cleared the Hook. I tried to calculate how much time there'd be before my absence would be discovered. Isabella usually brought me a breakfast tray at half-past seven. But Mrs. De Lancey and Mrs. Tryon didn't like to be woken until eight, or nine if they'd been to a ball the night before. They hadn't gotten in until late last night. Most likely they'd given orders for a late breakfast. Would Isabella dare disturb Mrs. De Lancey with news of my departure? Or would she choose to wait until her mistress was well rested? Either way, Isabella couldn't win. And poor Pepito, he was sure to be punished too. As much as I felt for Pepito, I was more worried that we wouldn't be far enough beyond New York to elude any soldiers or sailors who Mrs. Tryon might send looking for me, using her husband's influence. She might not be able to do that. Still, I'd feel better the farther we got from New York Harbor.

"How long will we be in New York's waters?" I risked asking Pruitt Jones when he seemed settled at the tiller and the boat was moving smoothly along.

He looked at me sharply.

"Will ye be pursued?"

I shrugged. Maybe my note would soften Mrs. De Lancey's feelings and make up for any injury to her vanity. Maybe there would be no pursuit.

"You didn't run off with the general's silver, did ye?" he asked.

"Indeed not!" I said. "In fact I left my mother's large pewter pitcher and my father's tankard to help repay my debts to Mrs. De Lancey." I had no intention of weeping in front of Pruitt Jones. But in spite of myself, I was soon awash in angry tears.

"Now, now, no need to get huffy," said Pruitt Jones. "We'll be past King's Point by midday if the winds hold. Why don't ye rest yourself on that canvas in the stern. You're looking peaked."

Peaked! I folded up Elspeth's shawl for my pillow and lay down on the lumpy canvas. I was so tired it felt as soft as eiderdown. Within moments I was asleep.

When I awoke, the sun was almost directly overhead. I was parched and sweltering in my dark woolen suit. I sat up, grateful for the breeze.

"Awake," said Pruitt Jones. "Thirsty?"

I nodded.

"Reel in that rope hanging off starboard."

It was a jug wrapped all around with coils of rope.

"Drink," said Pruitt Jones.

I pried out the cork and drank deeply of the sweet, cold water.

Pruitt Jones grinned. "That'll fix you up," he said. Nothing better than the spring by my back door."

"It's delicious," I said.

"Well, bring it here."

As clumsy as I felt, I delivered the jug without spilling a drop. Pruitt Jones took a long draught and handed it back to me. "We're almost in Horseneck," he said.

"*Connecticut!*"

"Aye," he said.

"We've truly left New York?"

He scowled and nodded.

I could have jumped up and done a little jig, except Pruitt Jones was looking so sour and preoccupied. So I kept all the jigging inside me.

"Keep a lookout for a cove," he said. "We've a little job to do before we're completely in Rebel waters."

"But shouldn't we keep going?" I didn't want to risk the slightest delay.

"I'm the captain, ain't I?" he growled.

"Yes, sir."

"So do as you're told."

I nearly saluted, but thought better of it. Before long, I did see a little sheltered inlet, and pointed it out to him.

"That will do," he said, and steered for it.

Our job was to clean off the black paint covering the name *Liberty*. Pruitt Jones handed me a rag soaked in spirits, and we both leaned over the prow and scrubbed. It was a nasty job, and difficult, too. But once the black was cleaned off, the letters shone brightly — *Liberty*.

"I'm not too keen to sail a Rebel boat," said Pruitt Jones. "But it's worse sailing a slipshod vessel."

My father's little dory looked beautiful to me. She had her rightful name back. Now that we were in Connecticut's waters, so did I.

"Right," said Pruitt Jones. "We're off."

We nosed back out to the open water, caught the wind, and were soon headed briskly for Fairfield. I'd gone out in the dory only a few times with Father and Uncle Seldon. I wasn't afraid of the water, but mother was. She preferred to keep me safe with her at home. That seemed like a terrible joke now. We'd all been "safe at home" when Mr. Thomas and the Tories came and destroyed all that. Anyway, I didn't recognize the coast, and didn't know how long it would take to get to Fairfield. The sun was moving slowly but steadily across the sky and began to dip toward the western horizon. I tried to be patient and not plague Pruitt Jones with questions, especially as he was looking increasingly grumpy. Or was it worried?

I followed his gaze eastward to the sail of a ketch bearing down on us. Pruitt Jones spat in the water.

"Pirates!" The word came out explosively.

Pirates! No. It wasn't happening. I couldn't be this close to Fairfield only to be dragged away again. Pruitt Jones got out his spyglass and studied the approaching vessel.

"Two sails, six men, two, maybe three guns." He wasn't talking to me, but I hung on his every word. "Odd name on the boat. Hard to read. The *Unco* — "

"The *Uncoway!*" I shouted. It was Eleazar Sherwood's boat.

"You know her?"

"Yes. She belongs to my father's good friend, Captain Sherwood."

"Even so," said Pruitt Jones. "She may not be a friend to us now. You keep still, missy. We'll hope for the best."

I was so excited to see someone from home, I wanted to wave my arms like windmills and shout, "Hallo! It's me, HOPE WAKEMAN!" But to please Pruitt Jones, my captain *and* rescuer, I sat on my hands and said not a word, even when the *Uncoway* drew alongside us.

I didn't recognize the three men standing in the prow. They were dressed like ragged Continental soldiers and looked mean. They might have been pirates.

Had these men stolen Captain Sherwood's boat? The one with the red beard spoke first.

"So we've found the Tory scum that took the *Liberty*."

"Things aren't always what they seem," said Pruitt Jones in such a mild tone that I hardly knew him.

The men laughed. It was the same kind of laughter I'd heard from the Tories just before they stole all our things and set our house afire. It sickened me.

Pruitt Jones laughed with them, as if there really was something funny. Then he drew a pistol out from behind his back and aimed it at the man with the red beard. The laughter ended. The two other men in the *Uncoway* drew their pistols, pointing them at Pruitt Jones. Pruitt Jones wouldn't hesitate a moment to shoot a pirate, especially a Rebel pirate, even if he died for it. But these men knew the *Liberty*. Maybe they *weren't* pirates. I could no longer sit still and watch. I stood on shaking legs in front of Pruitt Jones, facing the men's pistols.

"Sit down!" ordered Pruitt Jones.

I ignored him.

"This is my father's boat." I said it as loudly as I could, and it still came out rather pitifully. "Captain Jones is bringing us back to Fairfield. I am Hope Wakeman."

"Fool girl," said Pruitt Jones, "you'll be getting us both killed."

The men hadn't lowered their guns. But they seemed to be listening.

"This is Captain Wakeman's boat." I didn't know whether it was better to keep talking or to be quiet.

"Keep still," said Pruitt Jones.

So I kept talking. "You've no right to stop us. Please, put down your guns."

"Hope?" The man who'd been at the tiller, mostly hidden from me, stepped forward. "*Hope Wakeman?*"

"Captain Sherwood!" I cried. "You do know me, don't you?"

"Aye," he said, and a broad grin spread over his face. "We'd nearly given up on you! Yet here you are sailing the *Liberty* smartly home. Bless my soul!" He took out a large white handkerchief and blew his nose.

The men sheathed their weapons and smiled at me. I turned to face Pruitt Jones. "Put away the pistol," I hissed. He gave me such a sour look, but set the pistol down on a coil of rope.

I turned back to Captain Sherwood. "Tell me, please, sir. How fares my family?"

"They are well, Hope. All are well."

I had to hear it again.

"Mother?"

He nodded.

"Father? Jonathan? Mary and Abigail?"

"Aye. *All* are well, only sick with worry for you."

"Where are they?"

"Your mother and the children are with your grandmother in Litchfield. But your father . . ."

I knew it was too much to expect him to be with mother. "Is he still with General Washington?" I asked.

"No. Your father resigned his commission in the regular army to be closer to your family. Now he's a captain in Connecticut's militia. Hope, your father is in Fairfield!"

"What?"

"Are ye deaf?" said Pruitt Jones. "The man said Fairfield."

"I'm not deaf," I said. "I'm . . ." But I couldn't say another word.

"There, there," said Pruitt Jones, and he patted my shoulder gently. "You're happy, Hope Wakeman," he said. "What you are is *happy!*"

"Yes," I said. "What I am is happy."

21
Home

The *Uncoway* escorted us all the way to the mouth of the Mill River, in Fairfield, in case we came across real pirates in the Sound.

Though evening was coming on, Father was still working in the yard with some men, rebuilding our house. I ran up the path from the landing, straight for my father, shouting, "It's me, Hope! I'm home!"

Father dropped the awl he'd been using and caught me up in his strong arms. He held me so tightly, saying over and over, "Hope, my Hope!"

We cried and then we laughed. It was some time before I could explain anything. All I wanted was the safety of his arms. Eventually, Pruitt Jones took out his ragged handkerchief and blew his nose so loudly I became mindful of my manners.

"Father," I said. "This is Captain Pruitt Jones. He brought me and the *Liberty* back to you."

"Sir," said Father, taking Pruitt Jones's hand, "I am forever in your debt. You've returned my most precious treasure."

"Well, Captain Wakeman," said Pruitt Jones. "War or no war, 'tis foul business stealing a man's boat."

"Or his *daughter*," I said loud and clear. Now that I was home, I didn't have to choke back my every word.

Pruitt Jones turned a brilliant scarlet. Father laughed and hugged me. Then he hugged Pruitt Jones, which embarrassed the old sailor all the more. The happiness that began when Captain Sherwood told me that all was well with my family grew and grew inside me until there was room for little else.

That night we had a supper of thanksgiving with Uncle Seldon at the Perrys' house. I shared Prudence's bed, and we talked all through the night. Early the next morning, Father took Pruitt Jones and me to Litchfield. Captain Jones wasn't too keen to go further into Rebel territory, but Father insisted that he come so that Mother could thank him face to face.

Mother was more beautiful than ever I remembered her. She was still too thin, but now there were roses on her cheeks. She swooned when she first saw me. Father and I caught her, and soon we were all laughing, with tears cascading down our faces.

"Hope, my darling," she said, petting me as she would a babe. She looked into my eyes and seemed to see all the trouble I'd faced. "Thank you, dearest girl, for coming back to me."

The porcelain clock had survived intact, in spite of its travels and my clumsiness. Mother put it on the mantel in Grandmother Burr's parlor. It wasn't yet in its proper place. But soon it would be back on a high shelf in our new home.

Tick, tick, tick. It sang its gentle song. We were both safe.

Jonathan was round and jolly, so different from the fretful infant I'd left behind. He cooed and hugged me with his fat little arms, but he was most taken with Pruitt Jones. He seemed fascinated with Pruitt Jones's white beard and the holes and tears in his tattered clothing. I think Pruitt Jones enjoyed the baby's attentions, not that he admitted it. Mary and Abigail were quite shy with me at first. I was like a spirit returned from the grave. They both held back until I teased them some and bossed them some, which was more the way they remembered me.

Pruitt Jones lost all his gruffness when Mother took his weathered hand in hers and thanked him, her sweet face a study in joy.

"I wish you could've met Maude Thomas," he said. "She's the one really looked after your girl, until she . . ."

The story of my months away from my family took many days and long June evenings to tell. Grandmother Burr prevailed upon Pruitt Jones to stay with us, and, in his own way, he helped with the telling.

Everyone was appalled by the laziness and cruelty of Elspeth and the feckless behavior of Mr. Thomas. They were touched by the kindness and bravery of Mother Thomas. There was much sighing and more tears as I told the stories of Mrs. Doyle and her boarders, Mrs. Willows and the pox house. No one could believe the excesses of Mrs. De Lancey and Mrs. Tryon. But Pruitt Jones confirmed everything I said.

"Aye," he said. "Lady of Fashion, that one," and he might have spat except for being in Grandmother Burr's parlor. "A darned silly-looking woman."

"Still, I'm grateful Hope was taken in by *someone*," said Mother.

"But fancy Hope being in the house of a *British* general," said Father, and slapped his knee.

My favorite part was telling about jumping out of the window and climbing down the silver maple. The girls' eyes grew round and luminous. Nan and Martha squealed. Father just beamed.

"My *brave* girl," he said.

"And ye should have seen her stand up in front of that mariner's pistol," said Pruitt Jones. "Not many a man would have the gumption to do that."

They were all looking at me, as if I'd changed into someone else. "I was really scared," I said. "But . . ."

"But you did what you had to do," said Father.

"Yes," I said, and felt myself growing into the stronger, braver person my family saw.

Pruitt Jones stayed with us a fortnight. Then we all accompanied him back to Fairfield. Mother was anxious to see the progress on our house, to order new furnishings and attend to her kitchen garden. We had word that our house was partially built. We packed cots and enough supplies so that we could camp out in Fairfield through July and August.

Captain Sherwood agreed to take Pruitt Jones back to Oyster Bay. Before Pruitt Jones left, Father gave him two complete suits of clothing, and Grandmother Burr gave him Grandfather Burr's compass. But Pruitt Jones wouldn't accept any silver from Father.

"God willing," said Mother, "the war will end soon. Will you come back and see us then?"

"Aye," said Pruitt Jones. "I'd like you to meet the *Marianne*. She's the finest lady on the Sound."

It was my turn to say good-bye, but the words would not come, only tears as Pruitt Jones held my hand in his.

"There's no cause for blubbering," he said.

I nodded, but my tears continued. Here was this man who had been my enemy, who was now my friend.

He knew my story as no one else could. He had loved Mother Thomas, as I had, and lost her. I couldn't bear to tell him good-bye.

"Don't cry, missy," he said. "Your sorrowing is over."

He was right; my future promised happiness, except for the uncertainties of the war. And those, I knew too well, were great.

"I shall miss you," I said.

He cleared his throat and ducked his head.

"Will you visit Mother Thomas's grave for me?"

"Aye, that I will. I'll tell Maude you made it safely home."

"Thank you," I said. And I never did tell him good-bye.

Epilogue

At four A.M. on Wednesday, July 6, 1779, a few weeks after Hope's return to her family, two British men-of-war carrying some twenty-six hundred soldiers were sighted off Black Rock Harbor. Black Rock Fort sounded the alarm. At that point the intentions of the ships weren't clear. They had just come from plundering New Haven. Would they attack Fairfield, or pass it by? The ships seemed to be sailing steadily westward when they disappeared in a fog bank. But the lifting of the fog revealed the two warships anchored off McKenzie's Point, less than two miles from the town green. By midafternoon the small boats were sent to shore, packed with soldiers, ready for combat.

The militia set up a defense between the invaders and Meetinghouse Green. But they were easily pushed back by the formidable British forces, which included units of Hessians, Loyalists, and some of the fiercest and most skilled fighters in the British army. The militia retreated to a makeshift fortification on Round Hill.

Toward sunset, General Tryon ordered the burning of several houses. He then sent a message to Colonel Whiting, in charge of the militia, that Fairfielders who would remain at peace in their houses would be spared any harm to themselves or their property. The colonel replied that the citizens had already witnessed the unjust burning of their homes, and would continue to resist the British oppression. At that, General Tryon unleashed his forces and began the wanton destruction of the beautiful town. Many houses, barns, and shops were set afire. The air was harsh with smoke and flame; cannons roared continually as the ships blasted Black Rock Harbor and the defenders repaid them. From Round Hill and other points of skirmish throughout the town came the steady bark and crack of gunfire. Then the heavens assailed Fairfield with torrents of rain, thunder, and lightning. It was as if the Devil had come to claim Fairfield as his own.

At the first alarm, most of the citizens went to the hills for safety. A few women of some of the finest families in town remained in their houses, in hopes that they could prevail upon the British and save their homes. They were sadly mistaken. For what the British troops spared, vengeful Tories and the pitiless German troops destroyed.

The next day the British departed. Some thirty of their soldiers were buried in Fairfield. Ten Fairfielders were killed, some men were taken prisoner, and many were injured.

The path of destruction halted at the Mill River, but continued on to ravage Greens Farms. Ninety-seven houses, sixty-seven barns, twenty-eight shops and stores were burned to the ground. Two schools, three churches, the jail, and the courthouse were also left in cinders.

The Tory raid and the burning of Fairfield were only two of the many casualties in the birthing of the new nation, the United States of America.

With the surrender of General Cornwallis at York-town, October 19, 1781, the war was essentially over. However, the final evacuation of Redcoats from New York City didn't occur until November 25, 1783. Many Loyalists left with them, seeking sanctuary in Canada and England.

Author's Note

Nearly every summer day when I was growing up in Westport, Connecticut, I passed the statue of the Minuteman, which guarded the entrance to Compo Beach. No trip to the beach was complete without climbing on the Revolutionary War cannons pointed at Long Island against the Redcoat invasion. The Revolutionary War was all around me as I grew up, but I never paid it much notice.

Several years ago, my husband and I bought a house in next-door Fairfield. Very near to where we live is the old town center. Along Beach Road are several houses with plaques that date them before the Revolution and explain that these houses, where British officers were billeted, were among those very few spared when the British burned down Fairfield in July of 1779. In the nearby Fairfield Historical Society are pieces of furniture, small household items, and portraits of some of the people who lived in those houses. Their remains are buried in the cemetery behind Town Hall. Bulkeys, Hobarts, Tuckers, and Lathrops lie next to Wakemans and Burrs, names quite familiar to me. I went to school with Wakeman and Burr children, and bought cider at Wakeman's farm.

While exploring the history of Fairfield, I came across the story of Mary Palmer. After her home was plundered and burned, she was spirited away by the raiding Long Island Tories. Her neighbor, Captain Amos Perry, with his mate, Joel Hawkins, assembled a crew and set off in the sloop *Racer* to rescue her. They were successful. Later Joel Hawkins and Mary Palmer were married. Despite the happy ending, Mary's story was terrifying. The fact that people who lived just across the Sound, who no doubt were very little different from Fairfielders, could inflict such cruelty on an innocent young woman struck me. The enormity of the Revolutionary War became real to me.

Over two hundred years ago people just like you and me were caught up in a great struggle to create the United States of America. The war came right into people's homes and no one was spared. Neighbors fought against one another. Long Islanders raided the Connecticut coast, and men from Connecticut set off in whale boats to do similar damage in Long Island. In one famous raid, Connecticut Revolutionaries snatched Judge Thomas Jones, an important Tory, from his home during a party held in his honor!

Hope Wakeman's story is a fiction, although many true events and historical figures are woven through it. There was an Oliver De Lancey, who perhaps had a wife, though I doubt that she was anything like the character here. General Tryon really was responsible for the raid on Fairfield, but I don't imagine that his wife was in any way related to my fictional Mrs. De Lancey.

In telling Hope's story, I have taken certain liberties with the facts. In particular, I've exaggerated the difficulties of travel to and from New York. People did travel from New York to Connecticut despite the dangerous Bronx Cowboys and the terrible conditions of the roads. There is a tale of the era about a rutted and mud-filled New York road. A traveler comes upon a hat in the middle of the road. When the traveler lifts the hat, he discovers a man underneath it!

"Please, sir," he says. "Let me help you up out of the mud."

"Thank you, no," replies the man. "My horse is under me and I shouldn't like to abandon him."

In the telling of Hope's story, I've tried to be true to the spirit of the Revolutionary period, and to give modern readers a sense of the differing points of view during a critical time in our history.

Joan Elizabeth Goodman is the author of two other novels for middle readers, *The Winter Hare* and *Songs from Home*, as well as many picture books. She lives with her family in New York City and Connecticut.